Thorn

Macklins of Whiskey Bend, Book One
Contemporary Western Romance

SHIRLEEN DAVIES

Books Series by Shirleen Davies

Historical Western Romances

Redemption Mountain
MacLarens of Fire Mountain Historical
MacLarens of Boundary Mountain

Romantic Suspense

Eternal Brethren Military Romantic Suspense
Peregrine Bay Romantic Suspense

Contemporary Western Romance

MacLarens of Fire Mountain Contemporary
Macklins of Whiskey Bend

The best way to stay in touch is to subscribe to my newsletter. Go to my Website *www.shirleendavies.com* and fill in your email and name in the Join My Newsletter boxes. That's it!

Avalanche Ranch Press, LLC
PO Box 12618
Prescott, AZ 86304

Book conversions by Joseph Murray at
3rdplanetpublishing.com

Cover design by Sweet 'n Sassy Designs

ISBN: 978-1-947680-60-9

I care about quality, so if you find something in error, please contact me via email at shirleen@shirleendavies.com

Description

*He sought a different life. Now he's home.
As is the woman who left him without a
backward glance.
Can they put aside their past to forge a new
future?*

Thornton "Thorn" Macklin, ex-Special Forces
sergeant, has returned home to focus on his future.
Scorpion Custom Motorcycles is one of the two dreams he
pushed aside when he left Whiskey Bend. The second
dream? Well, it died long ago.

Grace Jackson works hard to be successful, trying to
forget the one great mistake from her past. Returning to
Whiskey Bend to work for the family business forces her
to confront her future—as well as the man who shattered
her heart.

Being close to his brothers, helping at the ranch, and
working with lifelong friends is exactly what Thorn needs.
The last person he expects to see is the woman who
vanished from his life without a word. Now she sits in her
plush office down the street, resurrecting emotions, as
well as memories he'd buried long ago.

Not only must he confront his feelings for Grace, he and
his friends face another danger. Someone wants their new

business to fail, and isn't above putting people at risk to achieve this goal.

Guarding against threats is what Thorn does best. Protecting his heart from the woman he's never forgotten is another matter.

Could coming home, and the hope of a second chance, be his ultimate journey?

Thorn, book one in the Macklins of Whiskey Bend Contemporary Western Romance series, is a stand-alone, full-length novel with an HEA and no cliffhanger.

Thorn

Prologue

Southern Afghanistan

U.S. Special Forces Sgt. First Class Thornton Macklin, Thorn to those who knew him, adjusted his heavy pack, bracing the rifle against his side. Including body armor, weapons, and batteries, his gear weighed over eighty pounds. Lighter than most days.

Summer temperatures had shot to over a hundred degrees, waves of heat radiating from the ground. Thorn didn't dwell on it. His thoughts focused on the men in his team and the crossroads they were sent to clear of enemy insurgents.

Today would be one of the last times he walked side by side with men he respected more than any others on earth. Men who'd become brothers, protecting each other's backs in hostile environments, keeping him sane when weaker men would walk away. Regardless of background, social status, or wealth, they were all the same when awarded the Green Beret insignia. They were his family, and his one regret when making the decision to leave the army behind and return home to Whiskey Bend.

Thorn never considered leaving the military, expecting to retire from the work he loved. The change occurred on a visit home during his last R&R. Within hours of arriving at the family ranch, his brothers, Del and Boone, delivered the news that a high school teacher, a mentor to them all, had passed away suddenly.

He and his brothers attended the memorial service, Thorn leaving with an overwhelming sense of loss. Not just for the teacher who'd believed in him, stood by him when his father didn't, but for the dreams he'd left behind. Dreams forgotten when Thorn made the choice to enlist and leave Whiskey Bend. He never regretted the decision, not for one single day, until the memorial service reminded him of what he'd once considered his true passion.

His decision resulted after painstaking thought, deep soul-searching, and not a small amount of whiskey. Old friends from high school gathered a few times after the service, admitting how it had moved them, reminding each one of the dreams they'd left behind. By the end of his leave, Thorn had boarded the plane with a new perspective and a determination to regain what had once been his dream.

He had no firm game plan, didn't know what his first move would be. For a man who'd lived and breathed Special Forces, the fact he had no clue of what came next didn't bother him. Instead, he felt exhilarated, prepared in a way he hadn't been at eighteen.

Glancing at the men flanking him, Thorn felt a twinge of regret, along with a renewed sense of purpose. As the trained soldier he'd become, he pushed both emotions aside, concentrating on the mission. One of his last.

Chapter One

Whiskey Bend, Montana
Several months later...

"It's been a long time."

Thorn looked up from the cup of coffee he'd been nursing at Evie's Diner, his face a mask. "Not long enough, Mr. Jackson."

Wolf regarded him for a moment, then gestured to the empty seat across from him.

"Go ahead." Thorn had no desire to spend time with Grace's father. They had nothing to catch up on. Nothing in common, as Wolf Jackson made clear to him on a stormy early summer night after high school graduation. Thorn could still feel the pain the man's scornful words caused all those years ago.

Crossing his arms, Wolf leaned back in the booth, studying the man before him. "I hear you were Special Forces." He motioned to the waitress for a cup of coffee.

"Not any longer."

"Heard that, too." Adding cream, he stirred it into the hot liquid, not taking his gaze off Thorn.

Thorn had been in too many situations where life hung in the balance to be scared of a man whose opinion no longer mattered. He had much to think about, none of which included the man sitting across from him.

"Are you looking for work?"

Jerking his gaze up, Thorn almost laughed. "If I were, I wouldn't be telling you."

Wolf didn't flinch, showing no emotion at Thorn's attitude. He deserved it. Much had changed since delivering what he knew would be a heavy blow to a young man he'd once considered a son.

"If you need help..."

Jaw tightening, he held Wolf's gaze. "Again, if I needed help, you'd be the last man I'd turn to." Standing, Thorn dug bills from his pocket, more than enough for two cups of coffee, and tossed the money on the table. "If you'll excuse me."

Turning, he straightened his shoulders, almost running into a woman entering the diner. Thorn paid no attention to her, settling his worn cowboy hat on his head, nodding as he continued past.

"Excuse me, ma'am." He heard a slight gasp, ignoring it as his hand hovered over the doorknob.

"Thorn?"

He almost missed the whispered word as he hurried to push the door open. Something about the voice made him stop, memories of a young woman racing through his mind. Turning around, his breath caught when she took a step closer. A vision from long ago returned. The same vision he fell asleep and woke up to almost every day.

Almost too stunned to speak, he forced a response. "Grace?"

Thorn couldn't move as she walked forward, taking him in, cataloguing the many changes. She reached up,

4

touching an old scar on his left temple, the simple action causing bittersweet memories to tighten his throat before he turned his head away.

Dropping her hand, she sucked in an unsteady breath, stepping away. "I didn't know you were back."

He glanced behind her, seeing Wolf watching, but making no move to leave the table. "It's been a few days." After the harsh words with her father, Thorn had no desire to speak with her. Not now, perhaps not for a long time. "I have a meeting. It was good to see you." Turning to leave, he stopped when her hand gripped his arm.

"How about we meet for coffee some time?" Grace didn't especially want to spend time with Thorn, but she needed closure. He owed her an explanation and an apology.

The wariness in her eyes almost had him wavering, forgetting the years it had taken for him to move on, dismiss his feelings for the woman he believed would always be a part of his life. The same woman who'd left him behind to follow her dreams.

Lowering his voice, Thorn looked down. "I don't think that's a good idea, Grace. Better to accept we've both moved on and leave it at that." He didn't believe a word he said, but it was what he needed to push her away, saving a small measure of self-respect.

Grace watched him leave, a deep sorrow seizing her as he disappeared down the street. Inhaling a slow breath, she chastised herself for caring. He'd walked out on her right after graduation. No explanation, no apology—nothing. It had taken a long time to reconcile the fact he'd left without her, tossing their plans out as if they were yesterday's garbage.

A few years later, she learned about the pact between her father and JJ Macklin. Her father's apology did nothing to soothe the pain Thorn left in his wake. They'd both been betrayed, yet it seemed she'd been the only one to grieve. In all those years, Thorn had never tried to contact her. He'd forgotten her as easily as he had Whiskey Bend.

Shifting her gaze to several empty stools at the counter, she didn't notice her father watching from a few feet away. Not that she'd care. Their relationship had long ago changed from a loving father and daughter to one of polite tolerance.

"What would you like today, Grace?"

"Coffee for now, Evie."

Leaning across the counter, Evie glanced both ways, her voice a whisper. "Wasn't that Thorn Macklin?"

Grace nodded.

"He sure has grown up, and in a very good way." Evie's eyes lit up. "When we were in high school, I thought you two would end up marrying. Then you both left town." Picking up a cup, she filled it with coffee before setting it in front of Grace. "I wonder if he's still single."

Grace had wondered the same, checking for and not seeing a ring on his left hand. "I'm sure he'll be back. Why don't you ask him?"

Evie held up her hand, wiggling her fingers to draw attention to a beautiful wedding set. "I don't think my husband would be happy hearing I'd been asking about Thorn's status."

The corners of Grace's eyes crinkled, although she found it hard to smile. "No, I guess not."

"But you're single, and if he is..." Evie raised her brows.

"Don't even think about trying to match us back up. What we had was over long ago. I certainly don't feel the same about him as I did at eighteen, and I'm sure Thorn sees me as nothing more than an old friend."

"Tell you what. You two come in together and lunch is on me."

Grace stifled a laugh, knowing it would never happen. "You can't do that."

"Sure I can. Remember, I *own* Evie's Diner."

A bell rang behind her. "Order's up."

Evie waved a hand at the cook. "Let me know if you want anything else."

"Hey, Grace. How are you?" Alley Cramer, a younger friend from high school, rested against the stool. Grace had always liked her, although they'd never had a chance to become close.

"I'm doing good. How's Shane?"

A huge smile crossed Alley's face. "What can I say? He's the best."

They both laughed as Evie walked up with the takeout order. "Here you are, Alley."

"Wish I had more time to stay and talk with you two, but..."

"Yeah, we know." Evie leaned a hip against the counter. "You have a growing man to feed."

They watched Alley leave, then Evie turned to grab plates filled to overflowing, leaving Grace to sort through her muddled thoughts. She had been away on a business trip during the memorial service a few months before, hearing Thorn had shown up with his brothers. By the time she'd returned, he'd flown back to base, saving them both from what she knew would be an awkward encounter.

"Grace."

Stiffening, she glanced over her shoulder at Wolf Jackson, a man who ruled his business and his family with a firm, unyielding hand. Much the same as Thorn's father had before he and his wife died in a fiery plane crash.

"Yes, Father."

He leaned against the stool next to her, not sitting. "You saw Thorn."

"Yes." Her hands tightened on the cup of coffee, readying herself for whatever warning he felt entitled to make.

Wolf sighed. It had been years since he'd heard any warmth in his daughter's voice. "Did he ask to see you?"

Swiveling on the stool, her gaze locked on his. "No, Father, he didn't. I asked him to meet me for coffee. You'll be pleased to know he refused." Shifting away from him, she hoped he'd get the message and leave her alone.

When he and JJ Macklin, Thorn's father, had made a pact to force the two teenagers apart, Wolf never believed his daughter would react with such cold loathing. He knew she'd be upset, rail against him, but her pain at what she saw as his betrayal had lasted fourteen years, since the day he'd sent her away. Confessing the truth had done nothing to warm her heart.

With Grace living across the country, both he and JJ had believed Thorn would bend to his father's will and, as the oldest son, take over more responsibilities at the ranch. Instead, the news of her leaving had propelled him straight into the army recruitment office. Within days, he was gone.

"I'll see you at the management meeting this afternoon?"

"Of course. Don't you always?"

Respectful, tolerant, and distant. If she weren't so good at her job, Wolf would be tempted to offer her a position elsewhere. "Yes, I do."

He waited for her to respond. When she didn't, he placed a hand on her shoulder, remorseful at the way her body tensed. Wolf opened his mouth to say more, then closed it. She'd shut him out. Dropping his hand, he nodded to a couple friends as he left the diner, pushing aside the regret of the pact he'd made. A pact he never should've agreed to.

"I heard you were back." Kull Kacey's gruff voice shot over his shoulder, his focus not straying from the custom motorcycle in front of him. "Thought you'd stop by before now."

Thorn leaned against a pillar in the garage that hadn't changed in all his years away. "Thought you'd be dead and buried by now, old man." Even in his late sixties, Thorn knew Kull was far from acting his age.

"Old man?" It came out as a good-humored growl. "I can still take you on, kid, and I wouldn't suggest you forget it." Pushing up, Kull held out his hand, gripped Thorn's, then pulled the younger man into a fierce hug. "You've been gone too long."

"Doing what I wanted."

"Step into the bar. I'll buy you a drink and let you whine to me about why you've chosen now to come back."

Thorn clasped his mentor on the shoulder, laughing. "Not on my worst day."

The garage stood behind Kull's real business. The one that allowed him to tinker with motorcycles, creating the most sought-after custom bikes in Montana. Wicked

Waters Saloon had been started with funds he'd saved from his days in the army, during his three tours in Vietnam, and had been a success since the day it opened.

He'd been married before he left for his first tour. When he returned from the last deployment, his house still stood as he'd left it, but his wife was long gone. No letter, no phone call, no message through a friend. A few weeks later, he received the divorce papers. Anger had pushed Kull to sign without a thought. He'd never seen the woman again.

In the following weeks, he'd sold the house and all he owned, climbed onto his Harley, and left Kansas, riding until he ended up in Whiskey Bend. A few months later, Wicked Waters became a reality and had been going strong ever since.

Filling two glasses, Kull pushed a whiskey and cola in front of Thorn. Holding them up, they touched the rims, toasting years long past. Settling himself next to Thorn, he leaned his beefy arms on the bar.

"Time to spill it, kid. Why are you back?"

"Mike Weiker."

Kull's brows scrunched together. "The science teacher? Hell, he's been gone for months. What's got you so riled up about his death that you'd quit the army and come home?"

Thorn rested his elbows on the bar and held up his glass, not sure how to explain the effect the memorial service had on him. "You know my father could be a hard case."

Kull nodded. "Yeah, usually in the extreme."

"No matter what, Mom sided with him, even when she knew he was dead wrong. That left me you and Mr. Weiker. I sought out your opinions, and you never failed me. Weiker dug into my life, offered to be a sounding board. Eventually, I took him up on his offer to talk."

"I thought you and Wolf Jackson got along well."

"So did I. Until he shut me out after sending Grace away." Thorn shook off the image of a stoic Wolf standing on his front porch, calmly telling him how his daughter had other plans. He'd refused to give Thorn a phone number or address. Not even a hint as to where she went. It had been a double blow, losing both Grace and Wolf at the same time.

"I heard the rumors. Didn't believe both you and that sweet girlfriend of yours had split up, going your separate ways."

"They were true, except for the part of us breaking up. She left without so much as a goodbye. Pop gave me an ultimatum—college or the ranch. He'd have been happy with either one. But I was smarter than him." He looked down at the glass in his hands, shaking his head. "Got up at dawn the next day and sat outside the army recruitment office until they opened."

"You stayed in my garage that same night, then crashed at your friend's house the next. Josh Reyes's, if I recall right. I never saw you again."

Thorn still felt the guilt of not telling Kull the truth. "The bus left early the next morning. I wasn't about to miss it."

"And the teacher?"

Thorn nodded at the bartender for a refill. This part would be harder to explain since he hadn't quite figured it all out himself.

"Weiker always encouraged me to follow my dreams. Listening to those who spoke at the service, it seems he'd done the same for any student who needed help. Most confessed how he'd gotten them thinking about their future and what they wanted to do, as opposed to what they thought they *should* do. Most hadn't followed their dreams, taking what they admitted was the easy way out. It got me thinking about my life, what you'd taught me and what Weiker had encouraged me to do. I glanced down at my dress uniform, feeling like I'd let myself, you, and Weiker down. The army was my escape, a way to get away from my father—and Grace abandoning me. For the first time, I realized it wasn't my dream. Not the one I wanted to follow for the rest of my life."

Tossing back the rest of his drink, Kull pierced Thorn with a hard look. "Let's get something straight right now. You never let me down. Not once. In fact, I couldn't have been more proud of you and what you accomplished." Pushing off his stool, he held up a hand. "Wait here. I'll be right back."

Kull lived in a beautiful home a couple miles outside town. His man cave—or personal retreat, as he preferred to call it—was above the saloon. A few minutes later, he came bounding back down, an album in his hand. Placing it on the bar, he opened to the first page.

Thorn's jaw dropped. Page after page contained pictures, newspaper articles, and personal notes scribbled in Kull's distinctive hand. Anything of importance that ever happened to Thorn had been preserved in a well-worn brown leather binder. From the time he first met Kull as a haughty twelve-year-old to a newspaper clipping showing the thirty-two-year-old Sgt. First Class in the crowd at the memorial service. It was all there.

"I left you a note when I came to town." Thorn wanted to make sure Kull knew he'd tried to see him during his last R&R.

"The one time I leave town for two weeks. Your timing stunk, kid." Chuckling, he clasped him on the back.

Thorn closed the book, laying his palm on top. "You kept everything. I don't think my parents ever considered making an album like this for any of their sons."

"Don't be too hard on them. They had a large, successful ranch to run and three rowdy boys. I had my saloon and garage, but no family. You became the son I never had."

Tears welled in Thorn's eyes, but he refused to let them show. Shifting away, he gathered his composure before looking back at Kull.

"Pop was a good man, but a lousy father. You were a good man, taking the time to understand the angry boy I'd become. The same with Weiker. Without the two of you, well..."

Kull whacked him lightly on the back of the head. "You'd have turned out fine without either one of us. You had your own journey to travel and I always knew you were meant to succeed. Your father just didn't take the time to see it." Sliding the book to the side, he leaned toward Thorn. "You've returned to follow your dream. Tell me what that means."

Chapter Two

Grace Jackson stared out her office window toward the activity down the street. Thorn had been back less than two weeks and already bought Kull's garage, working long hours with a skeleton crew to remodel the old building into what locals were already calling a showplace for custom bikes.

Scorpion Custom Motorcycles was scheduled to open in a few days and she hadn't yet worked up the courage to congratulate Thorn. Rumor was he intended to name it after Kull, but the older man refused. She didn't know if the rumor held any truth, but it sure sounded like something Thorn would offer and Kull would reject.

"They're making real progress."

Her curiosity at all the activity outside slipped at the sound of her father's voice. "Seems so."

Swiveling in her chair, she focused on the president and CEO of Gray Wolf Outdoors. Designing, manufacturing, and selling outdoor and extreme sports clothing and equipment, it had become a force with an expanding base in domestic and international sales. Grace knew she played a prominent role in the success, yet if a better offer came her way, she wouldn't hesitate to leave. Thorn's return just might be the kick she needed to speed up her search.

"Have you talked to Thorn or Kull since the work started?" Wolf moved closer to her desk, undeterred by the suspicious look on his daughter's face.

Her interest piqued. "No. Have you?"

"I talked to Kull last week. He sold it all to Thorn, although I suspect he'll still tinker around the garage when the urge hits." Wolf rested his hip against the edge of the desk, looking out the window. "Thorn has plans to expand. Did you know he bought the empty lot next door?"

Her eyes widened before she caught herself. Showing an interest in Thorn wouldn't be a good idea. Her father's apology had done nothing to stifle her belief he still saw Thorn as undesirable, too rough and edgy for his daughter. He'd never understand those same characteristics drew her to Thorn, still fueling a significant spark of desire.

"He must have big plans. No doubt he'll pile up a ton of debt getting it going." She fiddled with some papers on her desk, doing her best to hide her interest in anything related to Thorn.

"My understanding is he's doing it all with cash. The boy must've saved every dime he ever made in the army. Anyway, I didn't come here to talk about Macklin."

She sat up straighter, more than ready to move off the subject. "What is it you need?"

"I want to discuss our next phase of expansion." He pinned her with a hard stare. "You up to running it?"

Grace wouldn't have been more surprised if he'd walked into her office in a cleric's robe. Wolf had never given her the slightest indication he felt her ready to handle an expansion on her own. As Operations Manager, she'd worked on expansion teams, but never led one. She leaned forward, resting her arms on the desk.

"You know I can handle it or you wouldn't have asked. So give me the details and we'll talk about it."

"It's a central distribution facility in Texas, outside Austin. You'd be Vice President of Operations, in charge of all activities, with close to three hundred employees."

Her gaze narrowed. "Why Austin?"

"Cost, tax incentives, and a ready and willing workforce. We can recruit UT graduates for entry-level management positions, and the pool is strong for employees on the floor in distribution. You've been wanting to get away, so it seems like a good match for you and Gray Wolf."

She stilled at his words. Grace had been careful about her job search, keeping her desire carefully hidden from her family. At least she thought she had.

"Who says I want to leave?"

"Are you denying it?"

"You already know the answer. Now, please answer me."

Pacing to the window, he shoved his hands into his pockets. "You sent a blind résumé to a friend in another company. He didn't have an opening, but thought your skills matched Gray Wolf and sent it to me. It didn't take a genius to know you were the applicant."

"I see. So you're offering me what you think I want." Leaning back in her chair, she thought of all the reasons he'd want her to leave. A sudden thought struck her. One she didn't like. "Or is this another way for you to manipulate me into doing what you want?"

Wolf waved off her question. "Macklin is old news. You've made it clear you no longer have feelings for him."

Her feelings for Thorn were none of his business. What she needed to know was why her, and why now. "How long have you been working on plans for a facility in Austin?"

His face remained impassive. "Six months."

Resting her arms on the desk, she leaned forward. "That's a long time to be planning a major expansion without naming the lead person. Who's been handling the job to this point?"

"Does it matter? The executive team has decided to offer you the job."

Her irritation grew at his unconcealed attempt to handle her. The same way he'd handled her as a teenager. "It seems awfully coincidental for the job to be offered to me within weeks of Thorn moving back to Whiskey Bend."

Wolf flinched, ignoring her comment. "We need an answer within a week. You'd be provided with temporary living arrangements for up to six months." Walking to the door, he shifted back toward her. "It's a good opportunity, Grace."

"The glass company will be here in an hour to deliver the new windows. There should be enough daylight to get them installed today." Josh Reyes slid the phone back into his pocket, then climbed down the ladder. "Assuming you have the energy to keep up with the rest of us. I know you army guys run out of steam fast." Smirking, he slapped Thorn on the back.

Josh and Thorn had been best friends since meeting on the playground in elementary school. In many ways, the two were complete opposites, leaving many to wonder how they'd stayed so close all these years. Always smiling, having a personality that drew people to him, Josh had enlisted in the navy a few days after Thorn boarded the army bus and left town.

"I doubt a squid like you would know anything about stamina. I'm surprised you aren't already passed out in a corner." Thorn drained the last of his water, then tossed the bottle in the recycle bin.

"Neither of you know a thing about stamina. If you'd been a Marine—"

Thorn punched Tony on the right arm at the same time Josh whacked him on the left.

"Ouch." Tony moved away, shaking his arms in mock pain.

Thorn grinned. "You sound like a girl, Tony. So much for being a war-hardened jarhead."

Tony laughed. "As if a grunt like you would know anything about bullets and such." He bent down, grabbing a tool belt off a nearby chest. Strapping it around his waist, he raised his middle finger before walking back inside the garage. "*Oorah!*"

Josh laughed at their friend's antics. "Damn, it's good to have the three of us together again. I can't believe it's been fourteen years." He studied himself in the reflection of Thorn's sunglasses, rubbing his chin. "Do you think I look old?"

Thorn shoved him aside, shaking his head, a wide grin on his face. "I'm not paying you to screw around, squid. Get back to work."

Josh saluted before scrambling back up the ladder to the roof.

Although Josh and Thorn were tight right from the beginning, Tony had been the third member of the group, often tagging along on their escapades while growing up. Quiet and more cautious than either of the other two, Tony emerged from the Marines confident, with an attitude consistent with what he'd seen while deployed in Afghanistan.

"Just like old times."

Thorn whipped around, his smile fading. Grace stood a few feet away, her attention on the work behind him.

"Funny how the friends we make when we're young seem to stick." He winced the moment the words were out. Thorn had known Grace since grade school, too, believing she still considered Josh and Tony friends. His chest squeezed, wishing she felt the same about him.

"Yeah, most of them." She glanced at him, then stepped away, moving toward the garage entrance. "Father said you bought Kull's shop and the property next door. Congratulations."

"Thanks." He had no idea what to say to her, wasn't ready for the conversation he'd rehearsed for years. After all this time, demanding answers about why she'd left him after graduation seemed ridiculous. Yet not knowing felt as raw as it did back then.

"Hey, Grace. I wondered when you'd stop by." Tony set down the hammer, brushing off the dirt on his hands before wrapping her in a hug. "It's good to see you."

She touched his cheek before stepping away. "You'd see me more if you didn't hibernate at your folks' ranch."

"So true. Check out the inside." Tony made a gesture with his arm, glancing at Thorn as he followed them inside. "What do you think?"

"It's hard to tell with all the debris and stuff taking up so much space." She glanced over her shoulder, pleased Thorn had decided to stick around, even if he didn't contribute to the conversation.

"All right. I'll give you the tour. Follow me."

Listening to Tony describe the area where the bikes would be customized, Thorn knew he should head back outside. He needed to finish what he'd started before the windows arrived. His mind knew it, but his feet failed to move.

Grace had changed little. If possible, she was even more beautiful than he remembered. Hair the color of a raven's feather, long and sleek, fell to her waist. Her bright blue eyes danced with mischief as Tony pointed from one spot to another. Remembering when her eyes danced with passion, Thorn unconsciously placed a hand over his chest at the intense ache.

There'd been other women in the years since they both fled Whiskey Bend, but none had come close to Grace. Not in beauty, wit, or humor. And none had held a place in his heart—a heart that only wanted to beat for her.

"That's it. What do you think?"

Tony's enthusiastic voice drew Thorn's attention to the front, where the open framing waited for windows. Grace had stepped through the open space, looking back inside.

"I think it will be magnificent. You'll have more business than you can handle."

"Don't know if I can work long for the boss, though." Tony glanced over at Thorn. "Word has it he can be a real hardnose."

Grace chuckled, not moving her gaze away from Tony. "I've heard the same, but that was a long time ago. Maybe he's changed." Checking her watch, she stepped back through the window opening, giving Tony a peck on the cheek. "Thanks for the tour."

"You don't have to rush off." Tony slid his hands into his back pockets.

"I'm a woman on a mission. There's a sandwich at Evie's with my name on it."

As she left, Grace waved at Josh, who still worked on the new roof. Clutching her purse close to her side, she let out a strained breath. Thorn hadn't said more than a dozen words to her, which indicated he either still hated her or no longer cared. She'd guess it was the latter. Well, she no longer cared, either.

Congratulating herself on at least making an attempt to be friendly, she walked into the diner, glancing over her shoulder as she shut the door. Thorn stood on the sidewalk, his hands shoved in his pockets, his gaze still locked on her. His expression showed anything but indifference.

Evie greeted her, holding up a bag in one hand and a to-go drink in the other. "Thought you'd forgotten."

"I stopped by Kull's garage to see the changes."

"Those boys sure have made a lot of progress." Evie handed her the meal, ringing up the amount. "Guess you had a chance to talk to Thorn."

Pulling out her wallet, Grace paid for the food, shaking her head. "Tony gave me a tour while Thorn stood by and watched."

"He never was too talkative, even on his best days." The look Evie gave her hovered on pity.

Grace wouldn't let it bother her. Fourteen years was much too long to still carry feelings for any man, much

24

less one who'd taken off, never attempting to stay in touch.

"Guess I'd better get back to the office." She had no intention of returning to the office where her father would pester her about a decision. Instead, she planned to eat her lunch at Gray Wolf Park, taking her time, maybe not returning to work until morning.

"See you tomorrow, sweetie." Evie gave a little wave as Grace closed the door behind her.

Three blocks away, the land had been donated to the town by her father while Grace was in middle school. After the council voted to turn it into a park, she and Thorn used to hang out there to get away from their families, and Josh and Tony. Most times, they'd sit on the swings and talk for hours until one of them realized they had to get back home.

During football season, she'd meet him there after church on Sundays. All other days were reserved for practice or working at his family's ranch. Grace attended all his home games, plus as many away games as she could.

Taking a seat at a picnic table, she unwrapped her sandwich and took a bite. Grace used to love watching Thorn play. Josh was the quarterback, Thorn his favorite receiver, and Tony blocked anyone in their path. They'd won their division each year, coming close to winning the state championship twice. None of the three expected to play after they graduated, but they'd given all they had, collecting a bucketload of good memories to fall back on when times got tough. At least that was what they'd always told her.

Then they'd all left town. Who knew what they used to get through the ups and downs everyone faced. For Grace, anger at Thorn for leaving, then her father for lying, kept her going. Setting down the sandwich, she stared out at the creek skirting the park, realizing what a waste of time it had all been. Anger no longer held the power it once did. It had been replaced long ago with a healthy dose of disillusion and regret.

Dropping her head into her hands, she rubbed her temples. Maybe she should've been the one to track down Thorn, try to make things right. But she hadn't.

"Mind if I join you?"

She jumped, startled at the familiar voice. Twisting around, she saw Thorn a few feet away, a bag from Evie's in his hand. Pushing aside the lump in her throat, she gestured to the other side of the table. "Go ahead." Picking up her drink, Grace did her best to ignore him and the butterflies now lodged in her stomach.

Unwrapping his sandwich, Thorn couldn't seem to move his gaze away from Grace, studying her features for signs of the girl he once loved. Taking a bite, he chewed slowly, making her squirm under his intense gaze.

"Did you follow me?" She took another bite, but the sandwich now tasted more like cardboard than chicken salad.

"Nope."

She looked around, expecting to see Josh and Tony walk up any minute. Grabbing her drink, she took a long sip, deciding the best way to deal with him being so close was to talk.

"I eat here all the time. Two or three times a week, in fact. Sometimes there are families with children, but most days, it's quiet, like today. I've even brought my fishing rod a few times, although I've yet to catch anything. Seems the older I get, the less luck I have. I..." Her voice faded when she saw Thorn raise his hand.

"Do I make you nervous?" He wadded up the sandwich paper, easily tossing it into a can several feet away.

Grace crossed her arms, scowling at him. "Of course you don't make me nervous."

He mimicked her behavior, crossing his arms, although his lips turned up at the corners. "Then why are you babbling? I don't remember you being so chatty." Some perverse pleasure washed over him when he saw her face redden, her eyes going wide.

"It's called small talk, Thorn. It's what people do when they're trying to break the ice, be sociable. You should try it sometime."

He studied her a moment, his gaze hooded. "I've seen you naked, Grace. Several times. Do you really think small talk is necessary?"

Without an inkling of warning, she picked up her cup and threw the contents at him. Shock came in an instant, followed by disbelief, then a sputtering laugh as he stood, letting the liquid sluice off him.

Grabbing her trash, she tossed it into the can, then picked up her purse. "You're such a jerk, Thorn. I don't know how I ever loved you. Leaving here was the best decision I ever made." Her stomach twisted when his smile disappeared, replaced with something she couldn't quite define.

Standing, Thorn stepped beside her, leaning down to whisper in her ear. "You're right. My love would never have been enough for you. I'm all the things your father thought—and worse." Straightening, he adjusted his sunglasses and strode away, not bothering to check her reaction. If he had, he'd have seen the indignation of a moment before replaced with grief and regret, tears welling in her eyes at the love they'd lost and the pain that replaced it.

Chapter Three

"I never imagined the place could look so good." Kull stood outside Scorpion Custom Motorcycles, a bottle of beer in his hand, as he admired the new sign. Josh and Tony stood on either side of him. "You boys did real good." Tipping the bottle up, he took a swallow, hearing the deep rumble of an approaching motorcycle.

Josh didn't have to look to know who'd arrived. "Guess the boss decided to show up."

"Never a doubt," Tony added as they made their way through the crowd toward Thorn's Harley. They'd put off the grand opening until the bike had been brought out of storage and given a thorough inspection. Kull had helped Thorn trick it out while still in school, finishing a few months before graduation. He'd chosen basic black, deciding he needed it updated if it were going to be a bike representing Scorpion's talents.

The custom airbrushing had taken almost a week, but the resulting accolades were well worth it. Thorn and Josh had always been artistic. It was one of the common traits that brought them together—drawing motorcycles in pencil while pretending to be listening to their teachers. Josh had kept it up, taking a few art classes during high school and while in the navy. Afterward, he'd stayed in San Diego to work for a custom paint shop catering to wealthy clients. It was where he'd learned to perfect his airbrushing skills, adding his own touches when his boss would allow it.

Thorn had continued to draw, but shifted his designs to fabrication, learning all he could about motorcycle engines and repair from Kull. It had been his passion, as well as the wedge that caused the most friction with his rancher father. As the oldest of three boys, he'd been expected to take a leadership role at the Macklin ranch, which had been in the family for generations.

He'd done all his father asked, working long into the night after football practice and all day on Saturdays, fitting in time with Kull whenever possible. It had never been enough. JJ Macklin expected a hundred percent engagement by all his boys. He'd even gone so far as prohibiting Thorn from spending time with Kull. All the ultimatum accomplished was to put a serious dent in a relationship already spiraling downhill at a rapid pace.

"Wondered when you'd get here." Josh stepped away from the bike, crossing his arms and nodding. "Damn fine paint job."

Tony clasped a hand on Josh's shoulder. "I hear the guy who did it is for hire."

He smiled. "For a price, my man. A very *high* price. Speaking of which, at least five people have already put their names on the list for custom work."

Thorn swung his leg over the bike and surveyed the crowd standing around the large grill or next to the drink table. "Incredible turnout."

"Evie did a great job catering the food." Josh took another swallow of water, searching the crowd for the woman he'd crushed on all through high school. "We tried to help, but she shooed us away. Oh, almost forgot. You might want to check with your brothers, Thorn. They were looking for you." He indicated to where Del and Boone Macklin stood across the lot with a few other locals.

Adjusting his shades, Thorn took one more look around. "Guess it's time to mingle."

"Here he comes now." Delaware Macklin, Del to most, shifted his stance at the approach of his older brother. As the sheriff of Whiskey Bend, Del kept tabs on what went on in his town, going out of his way to attend the opening of every new business.

"Seems you're always running a tad late, *little* brother." Daniel "Boone" Macklin flashed a broad smile at Thorn.

"The day you can beat me in a fight is the day you can call me little, Boone." Locking an arm around his youngest brother's neck, Thorn emphasized his point before letting go. "How's the ranch work going?"

"Guess you'll find out this weekend. You *are* still planning to help out, right?"

"You know I'll be there. Whatever I can do to help, count me in. Del, you going to join us?" Thorn grabbed a bottle of water from the nearby drink table, twisting the top off and taking a long swallow.

"Yep. I've got deputies covering for me. With the grand opening, I didn't think you'd be able to make it." Del's well-worn cowboy hat sat low on his forehead. He'd worn it as far back as Thorn could remember, somehow getting the previous sheriff to approve him wearing it instead of the one authorized for deputies.

"Wouldn't miss it. Tony and Josh will be here."

Del raised his glass in salute. "It's good to see family still comes first for you, Thorn."

"Pop never thought so." Thorn shoved away the bitter memories, focusing on what he had before him. Del and Boone were his blood family. Josh, Tony, and Kull, plus those from his Special Forces team, were his chosen family. Overall, not a bad circle of people to have your back.

"Pop had his own way of thinking. He didn't like me becoming a deputy, either, and never understood we had our own dreams. We did what was right for us, including Boone." Del leaned closer, lowering his voice. "Before he and Mom died, Pop took Boone and me to dinner. He didn't say it outright, but both of us got the feeling our old man had regrets, especially with how he'd dealt with you."

Thorn snorted, shaking his head. "The only regret Pop had about me was that I enlisted, then re-upped for more tours. You stayed in town. Even with your job, you helped at the ranch whenever you could." He glanced at Boone. "You always loved it there. From the time he first placed you on a horse, we all knew you'd found your true love."

"Yeah, Boone definitely followed in the old man's image." Del clasped his younger brother on the shoulder.

"You're both right. Pop never rode me like he did the two of you. I never wanted anything more than to live at Rocking M, be a part of growing it." Narrowing his gaze, Boone swallowed more of his beer. "He never could accept that out of three boys, only the youngest wanted to be a rancher. The hardest part was he always believed you two were better suited to it than me."

Thorn studied Boone, confused. "Pop always knew you were the best rancher among us."

"No. He told you two and Mom that, but always contended I had a lot more to learn before I came close to being ready to run Rocking M. When the cancer came and he and Mom had to fly out of state for his treatments, he finally relinquished more control to me."

Del let out a slow breath, his face sober. "They knew Pop wouldn't make it. He had to move up the timetable for you to take over, Boone. No one considered the possibility of their plane crashing and us losing them both. We can't go back, change what was said or done. All we can do is move on, which is the reason we're here today." He grabbed a bottle of water, screwed off the top, and held it in the air. "To the success of Scorpion Custom Motorcycles."

"I'll drink to that."

Thorn cringed, recognizing the voice. He'd hoped Wolf Jackson wouldn't stop by, knowing he didn't approve of motorcycles or the man who owned Scorpion. Turning, he looked at the outstretched hand, knowing he couldn't refuse it.

Grasping Wolf's hand, he met the man's gaze, his face devoid of expression. "Mr. Jackson. I didn't think you'd have time to come by a small business opening like mine."

"I'm always available for an event like this, Thorn. Mind if I take a look inside?"

Thorn studied him, wondering what Wolf was up to. "Uh, no. I'll show you around. Del, Boone, I'll see you two later."

Wolf kept pace beside him, stopping a couple times to say hello to people he knew, taking in all the outside improvements.

After they stepped inside, Thorn motioned around the showroom. "As you can see, this is the main area where we'll display our finished work. Custom bikes will be placed in here until the owner comes for them. The rest will be our own bikes and those we build in the hopes of selling. The framed images on the wall are some of the work we've already done."

Wolf cocked his head. "I didn't know any of you had worked in this field before."

Thorn didn't doubt it. Wolf wouldn't have had a reason to keep up on any of them.

"Since leaving the navy, Josh has worked for a company providing custom paint jobs for bikes and cars.

Much of what you see on the walls is his work. Like me, Tony grew up on a ranch, tinkering with small engines, then graduating to cars and bikes. He's been a mechanic since leaving the Marines."

Wolf faced him, crossing his arms. "And what have *you* done, Thorn?"

The verbal slap had been expected. "You know me, Mr. Jackson. I slide through on the backs of others." Turning, he walked toward the back. "This is where the heavy lifting is done." Grasping the handle, he pushed open the door to reveal a state-of-the-art design and fabrication garage that would be the envy of most custom shops.

Wolf cleared his throat as he stepped in and looked around. "Impressive."

"We're already working on one bike and have requests for quotes on several more. Since we've no debt, I expect to be profitable within a few months." He didn't wait for a response before pointing to a glass-enclosed office. "This is the design studio. Using the CAD program, we'll be able to provide several designs, including 3D modeling. There's also an option for customers to go to our website and fiddle with the designs themselves, although I think the best use of that tool is for clients to provide their thoughts upfront so we can consider them from the start."

Thorn's mind continued to fill with ideas as he looked at the sleek setup, already anticipating the need for another designer. Someone Josh could train. He had forgotten Wolf stood behind him until the older man cleared his throat.

"You've put a lot of effort into this."

"Effort *and* money." And he wouldn't hesitate to pour more funds into Scorpion to secure his dream. "It's a competitive business, and we aim to be the best."

"There you are." Kull stepped into the room, walking up to Thorn and clasping his shoulder. "Great job, kid. Never a doubt in my mind you could make this happen." He sent a meaningful look at Wolf, daring him to disagree. "Tony is writing up an order as we speak, and Josh already has a meeting set up with the guy tomorrow. He owns some car dealerships up north and in Idaho. Wants one bike for himself and one for each of his site managers. I wouldn't even guess what the total for that order will be, but it will be a lot of change." Kull tipped the bottle of beer to his lips and took a long swallow.

"I won't get too excited until I see the client deposit in the bank. Guess I'd better get back out there." Thorn turned to Wolf. "Thanks again for stopping by. Help yourself to the food and drinks. Oh, and Kull, thanks again for using your alcohol license for this."

"Anytime, kid. You know I'll do whatever I can for you." Kull's gaze followed Thorn as he left, noticing Wolf had kept quiet. "What do you think of what those boys have done?"

Wolf took another slow look around, glancing out the window to the garage. "It's impressive. I'll let you know what I think of the business after a few months."

Kull looked at him. "You ever think it might be time to give the boy some slack? He's more than met most people's definition of a success."

"Maybe."

Taking another swallow of his beer, Kull focused a hard gaze on Wolf. "You're a hard man—always have been. It doesn't matter if you're dealing with family, friends, or strangers. It's what made you such a huge success. I just hope it doesn't come back to bite you."

Wolf's jaw worked, but he didn't respond before leaving Kull alone to finish his beer.

"Glad I stopped by today, Thorn. I happened to be in town, scouting a location for a new dealership. Your grand opening was an added bonus." Ian Hardesty grasped Thorn's hand, then turned to Tony and Josh. "I look forward to meeting with the two of you tomorrow."

"You're going to be real pleased with what we build for you, Mr. Hardesty."

Ian chuckled. "I've no doubt." He glanced at his watch. "I'd better get to my next meeting. If it goes well, Hardesty Motors will have a dealership in Whiskey Bend by the end of the year. I want to showcase one of the bikes in the showroom. You don't have a problem with that, do you, Thorn?"

Thorn did his best to hide his surprise. "No, sir. No problem at all."

"See you boys tomorrow." Ian left them standing next to each other, their excitement tapered by the crowd still milling around.

Tony nudged Josh with an elbow. "We are definitely celebrating tonight."

Thorn's attention went to a slim female figure walking toward them, a long black braid draped over her shoulder. "Do as much celebrating as you want, as long as you're both clear-headed for tomorrow's meeting. Excuse me."

Josh shot Tony a look as Thorn walked away to intercept Grace. "I hope our boy isn't making a mistake."

Tony shook his head. "Hell if I know what he's thinking. Wolf doesn't seem to have mellowed at all since we were in high school, and Grace left him without a backward glance. I love the girl, but wouldn't bet money on her."

Josh nodded. "Yeah. I hear you." He continued watching until Thorn stopped in front of Grace, spoke for a moment, then escorted her to the refreshments. "I hate to say it, but I sure wish she wasn't around. None of us needs the distraction of Thorn dealing with her a second time."

"We have to trust he knows what he's doing. In case you haven't noticed, he's not the same naïve kid who let her lead him around. Our man isn't going to be taken for a ride a second time."

Josh rolled Tony's comment around in his head as Thorn and Grace stepped inside the showroom. Taking a breath, he made his way toward a group of people, hoping Tony was right.

"This is where we'll place the finished bikes." Thorn closed the door behind them, then turned toward Grace. "I'm surprised to see you here. After the way you stormed off the other day, I didn't think you'd want to be anywhere around me."

Walking a few steps away, she turned to face him. "I don't hate you, Thorn." His deep laugh took her by surprise. Crossing her arms, she glared at him. "What's so funny?"

"You truly don't have a clue, do you?"

She blinked, confusion clouding her face. "I guess not."

His face sobered. "Forget it. Let me show you where we'll start all projects."

She didn't budge. "No. I want to know what you thought was so funny."

Shoving his hands into his pockets, Thorn shook his head, his face a mask. "Trust me. It wasn't anything."

At some point, he thought she'd mention her leaving, maybe even apologize or say she'd thought of him now and then. He'd gone through hell for months, not understanding what he'd done or said to make her walk away. Grace's avoidance today of any mention of their past told him all he needed to know.

"We can head back outside if you have no interest in seeing the design studio."

Dropping her arms, she let out a sigh. "I want to see the studio if you have time."

"I won't keep you long. I'm sure you have better things to do."

He turned away and opened the door to the office. Letting her pass in front of him, he did his best not to be obvious as he admired her slim figure and long legs, the way her hips swayed as she walked across the room. She'd always preferred dresses, and today was no exception.

Turning quickly, she smiled at him. "Like what you see, Thorn?"

Grinning, he took a step closer. "I always liked what I saw, Grace." Crossing his arms, forcing himself not to reach out and touch her, he leaned closer. "In the end, what I liked didn't really matter."

Her smile faded. She understood his meaning, knew she'd played a huge part in the accusation in his voice. She sat on top of the desk, not meeting his gaze.

"I know you want an explanation. For a long time, so did I."

Furrowing his brows, he cocked his head. "What do you mean you wanted an explanation?"

"There's so much—"

"Grace, it's time we left for Missoula." Wolf stood in the doorway. Thorn hadn't even heard him come in.

"Just a few more minutes, Father."

"Sorry. We needed to be on the road fifteen minutes ago."

Thorn straightened. "Thanks for coming by. When you have time, I'll explain about the rest of our plans."

Grace nodded, knowing they could never recover their past, hoping they might someday recapture their friendship. "I'd like that."

Chapter Four

"It's been several days, Grace. Have you thought about our offer?" Wolf sat behind the wheel of his large SUV, his eyes on the road, his thoughts on Thorn and his daughter. No matter what Grace thought, the company's offer of a vice president position in Austin had been in the works for months. Thorn's return was just what it seemed—an unfortunate coincidence.

She viewed the trips to Missoula with her father as a requirement of working for Gray Wolf Outdoors. He inserted himself into all aspects of the growing business, not hesitating to look over the shoulders of those he'd elevated to trusted positions. His own daughter wasn't excluded.

Most times, she made the drive alone in silence. The long stretches of road gave her time to think, plan her next move. She'd been looking to transition away for months, never suspecting her father knew of her plans. His announcement hadn't been as intriguing as he'd hoped. Instead, what she considered his machinations to control had only served to increase Grace's efforts to land a new job with another company in the outdoor apparel and equipment niche.

"Honestly, Father, with the new lines rolling out and increased hiring, I haven't had a chance to study the offer."

His hands tightened on the steering wheel. "You do remember I mentioned needing a decision within a week."

"If you're so anxious to fill the position, why not offer it to the person who led the expansion effort?"

Wolf chuckled, although his eyes showed no signs of humor. "That would be me."

She should've known. If it had been anyone else, she would have heard about it through the company grapevine. In her experience, secrets were made to be outed.

"Why wait so long to mention the move to me? You could've given me more time to make up my mind."

Glancing at her, Wolf thought of all the many opportunities he had to say something. Each time, another crises intervened, delaying the discussion. "You're right. I should've offered you the job weeks ago."

A knowing smile turned up the corners of her mouth. "I suppose Thorn coming home provided the kick you needed."

Gritting his teeth, he breathed in slowly, not wanting to say anything he'd later regret. "It's been fourteen years, Grace. Don't you think it's time to move on?"

She whipped her gaze to him. "Move on from what exactly, Father? You lying about why I was sent to live with relatives across the country? Or perhaps you lying about Thorn already leaving town without a word?" Seeing Wolf flinch gave her a small amount of satisfaction. "Maybe it's because you not only lied to a boy you professed to love as a son, but betrayed a daughter who

43

thought you walked on water. In your world, those actions may mean nothing. In mine, deceit isn't so easy to forget."

"I made a mistake."

Pushing aside the anger she thought had been dealt with long ago, she turned her head back toward the road, spotting the mile sign telling her fifteen miles remained until they reached Missoula. It couldn't come fast enough.

Grace loved her father, admired him in many ways. Starting with nothing, and despite all the naysayers, he'd taken a dream and made it a reality. By the time she entered grade school, Gray Wolf Outdoors was a success. Their products now sold out of their own locations, as well as sporting goods stores and a well-known discount merchandiser. As Operations Manager, she'd toured every facility, knew the employees by name. In that part of her life, it felt good to be a Jackson. She still had work to do on the personal side.

"So you've said, Father."

A look of regret claimed Wolf's normally stoic features. "Are you hesitant to take the offer because of Thorn? Do you still love him?"

She couldn't tell him the truth. He'd only increase his efforts to discredit Thorn and the hard work he'd done in the army and now with opening his own business. She refused to be the cause of more animosity.

"Of course not. It's the knowledge you lied to me the way you did and believed it wouldn't affect our relationship. And it's the possibility you might do it again in order to manipulate me."

"You think the position in Austin has to do with control?"

Sighing, she gripped her hands in her lap. "I don't know."

"The offer has nothing to do with Thorn and even less about manipulating you. You're the best person for the job, Grace. That is the only reason behind the proposition. Well, and the fact I don't want you leaving Gray Wolf entirely. You've done a fine job and have a real chance of running the company someday. Austin is the ticket you need to punch for others to take you seriously."

"The Advisory Board." Grace had always fought to be recognized within the powerful group of advisors her father had assembled. Most were local and close to his age. A couple had come from the outside—younger, intense, without the loyalty Grace expected from those guiding the company. More than once, this second contingent voiced recommendations to sell the company to one of the larger competitors. Wolf and his cohorts had held firm.

"Correct. They've noticed your hard work, what you've accomplished. Still..."

"I'm your daughter and they don't want it to appear as nepotism."

"And neither would you." Flipping on the signal, Wolf turned into their Missoula location. Stopping the SUV, he shifted toward her. "We're meeting with a couple guys who are making innovative changes in outerwear. I've been in talks with them for about three months. This is the first time we'll meet in person. You're my second set of eyes on this, Grace. If these boys are as talented as I believe them to be, a licensing agreement could take us to the next level."

Reaching behind her, she grabbed her laptop from the back seat and got out. Leaning over the hood of the car, Wolf stared at her. "You've got one more week to make a decision about Austin, Grace."

One more week, she thought, following Wolf inside. Taking the position would give her the ability to show her full capabilities. Not taking it would secure her a spot in middle management for a long time, maybe forever. Few got far at Gray Wolf if they bucked the desires of the president, and no exception would be made for his own daughter.

Whiskey Bend

"Nice ride." Josh walked around Thorn's tricked out Harley, nodding his approval at the completed design. An hour after the grand opening closed down, Thorn had exchanged his customized everyday ride for the finished product sitting before them.

Swinging his leg over the seat, Thorn lifted his sunglasses to rest on top of his head, placing an arm over Josh's shoulder. "Nice? Hell, it's insane."

"Should be. It took us long enough to get it perfect for you." Stepping away, Josh admired the work the three had put in on the bike over the last couple weeks. "It should be in the showroom."

"That's my intention. I want Hardesty to see it at our meeting tomorrow. The examples he saw are great, and got him to sign, but this one..." Thorn shook his head, admiring the changes they'd made.

Burnt orange covered the metal, Josh's stylized Celtic knot scorpion wrapped around the tank, front, and rear fenders. Two metallic golden pincers curled toward the gas cap, the stinger poised and ready to strike at the V of Thorn's thighs. The handlebars curved in a perfect arc toward him, the instrument panel enhanced with metallic burgundy and black.

A similar scorpion graced the sign above their building, as well as on shirts and hats sold inside. They planned for all their motorcycles to sport a smaller image, a signature of sorts to memorialize the custom nature of each bike.

"Looks like we may have a late arrival."

Thorn followed Josh's gaze to a newer black truck, a good deal of chrome accenting its lines. A large man, a little overweight with thick arms and a barrel chest, emerged. Yanking up his pants, he started toward them.

"You the owners of this place?"

Thorn glanced at Josh, seeing Tony walking toward them from the shop. "We are. I'm Thorn, this is Josh, and Tony is right behind." He held out his hand.

Grasping it, he nodded at the other two. "Crayton Jones." His eyes narrowed at Thorn. "You aren't one of JJ's sons, are you?"

Thorn stiffened as he studied the man's face, trying to recall if he'd ever met him. "I'm the oldest. You knew my father?"

Jones stepped closer to Thorn. "I can see the resemblance. Sorry to hear about what happened. He was a good man."

"How did you know him?"

"Fought in Vietnam together. Your old man saved my butt more than once."

Thorn's gaze narrowed on Jones. His father never spoke of the war, and as far as he knew, didn't keep in touch with any of the men who fought with him. Del had come across a few medals once, scooping them up and dashing outside to ask JJ about them. Without a word, their father had taken them from Del's hand and stormed back into the house. They'd never seen the medals again.

"He didn't talk about the war."

"Can't blame him. Most of us don't." He glanced over his shoulder at the shop. "Good-sized place."

Nodding, Thorn gestured toward the showroom. "Would you like to see inside?"

"Sure would. First, I'd like to look at this bike. You boys build this?"

"It's a customized Harley. We break them down and rebuild them using the owner's ideas—or come up with our own design. Usually it's the latter. This is one of the more elaborate bikes. We just finished it last night." Thorn couldn't help the pride he felt each time he looked at the beauty before him.

"Mighty fine work." He leaned over the bike, running his hand over the gas tank. "Don't think I've ever seen such a fine paint job. Did one of you do it?"

"Josh designs all the finishes."

"You're quite an artist."

Josh stepped closer. "Thank you, sir. Why don't I show you around inside."

Thorn and Tony watched as they walked into the showroom and closed the door.

"What do you think?" Tony asked, crossing his arms.

Thorn lifted a brow. "About what?"

"Crayton Jones. He seem legit to you? I mean, do you think he knew your father?"

Shaking his head, Thorn turned his attention to the man's truck, noting the Wyoming license plate. He wondered what business the man had in Whiskey Bend and what brought him to stop at Scorpion.

"Could've fought with him. My father was in the army and did fight in 'Nam. I don't know much beyond that. None of us do."

"I have a strange feeling, Thorn."

Chuckling, he placed a hand on Tony's shoulder, his tone somber. "If I've learned nothing else, I've learned to respect your feelings. Do you want to talk about it?"

"Ah, shut the hell up, Thorn. You know what I mean."

Dropping his hand, Thorn had to admit he did understand. "Yeah, I do. He'll probably take off today and we'll never see him again. Let's make sure everything's secure so we can close up when Jones leaves. We've got a big day tomorrow."

The house Thorn rented in town dwarfed the living quarters he called home over the last fourteen years. Even after a month back in town, two bedrooms and two baths were a luxury he hadn't quite grown accustomed to.

Picking up a plate of reheated spaghetti and a cold bottle of beer, Thorn settled into a chair, using the remote to surf channels. He'd known of the various survivor-type shows, seen a few episodes, unable to see the fascination. If people wanted to learn to survive in hard conditions, they should enlist. Any of the branches would be happy to show them how to survive in miserable conditions with bullets coming at you from all directions.

Surfing through local news, domestic news, and sports, he settled on a classic movie set in the old west.

Tipping back the bottle, he took a long swallow, then dug into his dinner. It had been a good day. The grand opening exceeded their expectations. The fact they wrote up several orders pretty much guaranteed work for a minimum of two months.

Setting his empty plate aside, Thorn relaxed in the overstuffed chair, taking another long swallow of beer. Tomorrow, and all the days following, would be long. A smile tipped up the corners of his mouth when he thought of Mike Weiker and all their long talks after most students had left campus for the day. Football practice cut into their time during each fall, but the teacher somehow always found time for him. And for Grace. And for who knows how many other students over the years.

Although Thorn missed his Special Forces team, the feeling of accomplishment by returning to the dream he and Weiker talked about felt damn good. A lot of work remained, but he couldn't help the enthusiasm at getting this far so soon.

Closing his eyes, Thorn's thoughts turned to Grace and their brief conversation. She'd looked good today. Better than good, if he were being honest. He had a hard time reminding himself he no longer had the right to feel anything for her. She'd made it clear their time had passed when they took different paths all those years ago, although one comment stuck in his mind.

Grace mentioned she wanted an explanation of what happened. Her comment intrigued him, but there'd been no opportunity to ask questions before Wolf walked in, ushering her out. Well, Thorn wanted an explanation, too. No matter how long it took or how hard he had to push, he would discover why she'd left and why her father had turned against him.

Joining the army had changed him. He'd grown up, no longer running as he did at eighteen. He meant to make Whiskey Bend his home and Scorpion Custom Motorcycles a success. To do both, he had to put the past behind him, and he meant to do it sooner rather than later.

Missoula

Grace sat across the restaurant table from the two young men whose product design concepts could propel Gray Wolf Outdoors to new heights. Wolf had been even more impressed than her, asking questions and making suggestions in an animated fashion she hadn't seen from him in a long time. Not only did he like the designs, he'd established an instant rapport with the owners of the boutique firm—brothers who'd bootstrapped their business right out of college.

Dinner had gone well. The prototypes they brought had Grace already considering ways to market the specialized vests.

Checking the front and back before sliding down the zipper to study the inside, she counted the various pockets. She liked the fact the material was lightweight, windproof, waterproof, and breathable, knowing it could be used for all the designs she envisioned.

Wolf leaned back in his chair, a satisfied expression in his eyes as he followed the way Grace worked with the two young men. Finalizing the meeting, the brothers agreed to have updated prototypes and a proposal to Wolf by the following week.

After brief goodbyes, Grace followed her father outside and climbed into the SUV. She had to give him credit. He could identify talent. The brothers had submitted their ideas to several outdoor product firms, Wolf being their sole response. He'd always been able to keep ahead of the competition, and it appeared his winning streak would continue.

As they turned onto the road toward Whiskey Bend, she found herself hoping Wolf wouldn't push her any further about the job offer or Thorn. Neither was a subject she wanted to discuss with him tonight.

"You look tired." Wolf glanced over, concern showing on his face.

Shrugging, she settled back against the seat. "There's been a lot going on."

They rode in silence for several minutes before Wolf spoke again. "I'm sure it's not easy having Thorn back in town."

The lump in her throat came as a surprise. Thorn had turned into everything Grace imagined when they were teenagers. Confident, smart, accomplished. He'd also matured from a good-looking boy into an incredibly handsome man. She'd seen the way women watched him at the grand opening. The same kind of looks he'd received from girls in high school, except now, the women showed an aggressive hunger Grace hadn't expected. The thought of him taking any of them up on their undisguised interest caused her stomach to churn.

"He's been a complete gentleman since his return." Unless she counted his comment at the park about seeing her naked. Although she'd acted offended, his words and the heat in his gaze had triggered a flash of desire so strong, she'd felt her body sway. He always had an intense effect on her. After all these years, she'd yet to meet another man who intrigued her, setting off all her senses. Her denials meant nothing. Grace was still in love with Thorn, and doubted another man could wipe him from her memory.

Wolf sighed, his focus on the stream of traffic moving toward them. "From what I remember, he always treated you well."

"He respected you, looked up to you, sometimes more than he did his own father. I'll never understand how you could turn on him so quickly." As soon as the words were out, Grace wished she could drag them back. She didn't want to get into it tonight. Letting out a breath, she looked at Wolf. "Never mind. It isn't something I want to talk about."

Respecting her wishes wouldn't be hard. Wolf didn't have an answer for Grace, other than he'd been swayed by JJ Macklin's arguments, his need to have Thorn focus on his responsibilities at the ranch, not on some high school crush. Wolf believed they had been too young to commit, but he wouldn't have pushed them apart without the unrelenting pressure from the elder Macklin.

In the end, they'd all lost. Grace and Thorn were torn apart, him turning his back on his father the same way Grace had on Wolf. The difference was he still had a chance to improve the strained relationship with his daughter. Thorn would never have the same chance with JJ.

Severe regret pulsed through Wolf, seeing what a fine man Thorn had become and how Grace still looked at him. It was the same look Wolf's wife still gave him. His heart broke knowing he'd taken such a precious gift away from his daughter. If only he could turn back time.

Chapter Five

"You've got to get here right away. The flames are growing. I've already called it in." Josh's rattled voice came through the phone loud and clear.

"I'm on my way. Don't go inside."

Thorn went into what his army brothers would call "combat mode". Within minutes, he jumped into his truck. He hadn't asked any questions when Josh called, so he had no idea what he'd find. Rounding the last corner, he counted two fire trucks and at least a dozen men working diligently to extinguish the remaining flames. Screeching to a stop outside the barriers, he dashed past two police officers he knew from high school, meeting Josh and Tony on the street in front of the garage.

Tony placed a hand on his shoulder. "It's not as bad as it looks. The fire department was already on the way when Josh called."

"The monitor system you insisted on installing probably saved the shop. I got a call within minutes of the alarm going off." They had designated Josh as the main contact for the alarm company.

Thorn watched, his heart slowing as he took in the damage. "Appears to be concentrated in the storage area."

Tony nodded. "Looks that way. We can reorder the materials as soon as we inventory the loss."

"Any idea how it started?" Thorn paced a few feet closer, backing up when one of the firefighters held up his hand to warn him off.

"Not yet. They've called the arson investigator from Missoula. Seems we don't have one in town. Hold on." Josh reached into his pocket, pulling out his vibrating phone. "Reyes." His eyes grew wide, his jaw muscles twitching. "Who the hell is this?" Shifting quickly, he scanned the crowd, looking for anyone with a phone in their hand, then let out a series of curses when the line went dead.

Thorn turned toward him. "What's going on?"

"I believe it was the person who started the fire. Sounded like a man. Said something about the town not wanting us here."

Thorn's gaze hardened, his face a mask. "Any chance it could've been a kid?"

Josh shrugged. "Anything's possible, but the voice sounded older to me. It didn't sound like he used a voice changer."

"Damn it all." Tony rubbed the back of his neck. "We've got the meeting with Hardesty this morning. Should I call him to reschedule?"

Thorn didn't hesitate. "No. Assuming it's arson, whoever did this is trying to push us out. We won't let that happen. Hardesty comes in as planned." He looked at Josh. "Go find whoever's in charge and tell them about the call. They might be able to track it."

"Who's the owner?"

They turned to see a man in uniform standing behind them.

Thorn held out his hand to the older man of average height, permanent lines of worry marring his face. "We're partners. I'm Thorn Macklin."

"Yeah, Thorn. I know your brother, Del. I'm Detective Rick Zoeller. I've just spoken with the fire chief. It appears the fire was deliberate."

"Josh just got a call from someone claiming responsibility." Thorn glanced at Josh. "Show him the number."

Taking it from his pocket, he held it out to Zoeller. "The last number that came in."

Rick took the phone. "I'd like to talk to the three of you while they're mopping up. We can go over by my car. It shouldn't take long."

"What's going on?" Grace sat up straighter in her seat, looking out the SUV window. "My God. It's Thorn's shop. Stop the car."

"There's nothing—"

"*Please*, Father."

Pulling over to the side, Wolf kept the engine running as Grace jumped out, sprinting toward the barricade. Stopping, she scanned the area for Thorn.

"Grace. Over here."

Turning, she saw Tony motioning to her, Josh next to him, and Thorn in deep conversation with another man. When he turned, she groaned, recognizing Rick Zoeller, a man she'd begun seeing a week before Thorn came back to town. Jogging up to them, she stopped beside Thorn.

"Is everyone all right?"

Thorn's features softened. "We're fine, Grace. A little fire in the storage area."

Closing her eyes, she nodded.

"I thought you were in Missoula with Wolf."

"We just got back and I saw the fire trucks." She looked past Thorn to the detective. "Hello, Rick."

"Grace. You know these three?"

"All my life. We went to school together. Do you know how it started?"

Rick moved from behind Thorn. "Fire Chief thinks it might be arson. We'll know more when the investigator from Missoula gets here. You look tired."

Snorting, she rubbed a hand across her forehead. "That's what Wolf said not too long ago." She glanced at Thorn. "There's been a lot going on."

"Well, not much more to discuss until we get the report from the investigator. As soon as he clears the area, you can start cleaning it up." Rick stepped next to Grace. "We still on for tomorrow night?"

Thorn's eyes flashed at the question, his features unreadable.

"Uh, yes. Tomorrow is fine."

"Great. I have a surprise for you." Turning back to the others, Rick pulled business cards from his pocket and handed them out. "Call me if you find anything or think of something. You never know what small detail will help. I'll walk you back to your car, Grace."

She opened her mouth to protest, then closed it. Now wasn't the time to talk with Thorn. Even if it were, she had no idea what to say with Rick beside her. They weren't serious—at least she wasn't. He might not agree.

Tony crossed his arms, cocking his head. "Well, it appears Grace is seeing the good Detective Zoeller."

Thorn's jaw tightened, but he didn't respond. Who she dated had nothing to do with him. "Let's see if they'll let us take a look at the damage."

A couple minutes later, the three stood around the perimeter of the building, looking in through windows. They wouldn't be allowed inside until after the investigator finished the following day.

"Doesn't look too bad. A few boxes in the corner." Tony walked to the other window. "Looks like that's it."

Josh turned to Thorn. "Could've been a lot worse."

"Or it could've put us out of business for weeks." Thorn didn't like the idea of being targeted. The fact someone could've gotten injured or killed set his blood boiling.

First, he needed to neutralize the threat, find out who did this and stop him from trying again. Discovering the reason for going after them could wait.

"There's no sense in all of us waiting around for the arson investigator. Why don't you two head home?" Thorn walked to the front entrance, using his key to enter and check the showroom. Seeing nothing out of the ordinary, he closed the door and turned, almost running into Josh.

"I'm going to stay a while. I'd like to hear what the guy has to say."

"I'm with Josh." Tony stepped up beside them. "I think we need to meet the guy who's doing the investigating."

"Are one of you Thorn Macklin?"

All three turned at the sound of the husky feminine voice. Gray slacks, long-sleeved blue shirt, and sturdy black shoes couldn't disguise her flattering curves, nor detract from her gleaming red hair and sparkling blue eyes. Clearing his voice, Thorn stepped forward, extending his hand.

"I'm Thorn Macklin."

She clasped it, then let go, offering him a card. "I'm Jillian Somerville, the arson investigator." She saw his eyes widen, hearing groans from the men behind him, and sighed. "I know. You were expecting a man."

"Uh, no, ma'am. Well...maybe. Anyway, it's good to meet you. This is Josh Reyes and Tony Coletti, my partners. Where would you like to start?"

"Believe me, I know what it's like to deal with interruptions to business." Ian Hardesty walked into the storage room, surveying the damage. "This doesn't seem too bad. I'll bet you'll have it fixed up with replacement material within a couple weeks."

Thorn stood behind him. "Two days for the repairs and four for new material. It won't slow us down on your orders."

After Ian arrived, they spent two hours discussing designs, with Josh preparing sketches, and Tony inserting his thoughts on mechanical changes. Ian wanted five distinct bikes, all to be ready the same day and delivered to his five locations.

Ian glanced at his watch. "Before I leave, how about lunch? I saw a diner down the street."

"Evie's, but it will be on me."

"I won't argue that." Ian fell into step next to Thorn. "I heard you were in the army."

"I was."

"Special Forces?"

Thorn pushed open the door of the diner, standing aside to allow Ian to enter. "Yes, sir. Got out a few months ago and came home." When Thorn caught Evie's attention, she motioned toward an empty booth. Removing his cowboy hat, he sat down.

Taking a seat across from him, Ian rested his arms on the table. "Had enough, huh?"

Thorn considered the question a moment, wanting his answer to be accurate. "No. I had planned to re-up. Changed my mind when I came home during R&R. That's when I decided to follow the dream I had in high school."

Ian picked up a menu, the corners of his mouth tilting up. "Open a motorcycle shop?"

"No, sir. Open the best custom shop in the Northwest."

Nodding, Ian finished scanning the menu and set it down. "I know the feeling. Owning and selling cars is all I've ever wanted to do. And I wanted to have more dealerships up north than anyone else. My dad thought I was crazy. He refused to help me unless I got a college degree."

"What did you do?" Intrigued, Thorn leaned forward.

"Same as you. I enlisted, saved all my money, and opened my first dealership when I got out."

"No kidding. Army?"

"Hell no. Marines." Ian smiled. "Oorah."

Conversation stalled while they ordered, giving Thorn time to mull over what he'd learned about Ian. Everyone had heard of Hardesty Motors. He'd always assumed it had been around for generations. Looking across the table, Thorn guessed Ian to be maybe fifteen years older than him. Mid-to-late forties. As if reading his mind, Ian cut into his thoughts.

"I'm almost fifty, and it's been a wonderful ride. There's been no time to second-guess my decision. Even if I did, it wouldn't change a thing." Lifting the coffee to his lips, he took a sip. "Give it some time. I'm betting opening Scorpion will be the best decision you've ever made."

"The guys on my team were tight. It's the same with Josh and Tony. We grew up together, always had each other's backs. It hasn't been too bad." Thorn chuckled. "Actually, it's been pretty damn good so far."

Evie set their food in front of them. "Anything else, gentlemen?"

"That's it for now, Evie." She turned to leave, then Thorn's voice stopped her. "Evie, this is Ian Hardesty. Ian, Evie Denton, owner of the best diner in Whiskey Bend."

Evie tilted her head, studying him. "Any relation to Hardesty Motors?"

Ian smiled. "One and the same."

"Good. Hope you're talking about custom bikes with Thorn 'cause he and the boys are going to rock the Northwest with their designs."

Ian laughed, glancing at Thorn. "You've got a real fan." Looking back at Evie, he nodded. "As a matter of fact, I've ordered more than one. And I agree with you. Scorpion's going to be a big deal real soon."

Satisfied, Evie walked away, her hips swaying.

"She's a firecracker."

Chuckling, Thorn nodded. "Yep. Has been since high school."

Turning at the sound of the bell over the entry door, Thorn's throat tightened at the sight of Grace, her hair in a sleek ponytail. Spotting him, her eyes brightened before she looked away.

"Friend?" Ian took a bite of his burger, brow lifted.

Thorn turned back around. "Yeah...since high school. Her family owns Gray Wolf Outdoors."

"Must be Wolf's daughter."

"You know him?"

Ian nodded. "Acquaintances. We've worked on a couple statewide committees. He's built quite the business." Finishing the burger, he sat back, his gaze moving to Grace. "He mentioned a daughter, but I've never met her. Does she work for him?"

"She does." Thorn stared at his half-eaten sandwich, not interested in the rest. "I'd better get back to the shop. We have a lot to get done to meet your deadline." Reaching into his pocket, he pulled out a credit card.

"Save it, Thorn. I know you offered, but this one's on me." Ian tossed a fifty on the table and stood. "I'll be back in town in two weeks." Shaking Thorn's hand, he waved at Evie before walking out the door.

Picking up his glass of soda, Thorn walked to the counter, settling onto a stool next to Grace. Twirling the ice around in the glass, he waited until she looked at him.

"Hope I'm not taking someone's seat."

Lifting a brow, she looked behind her, then back at Thorn. "I don't believe so."

"Like your boyfriend, the detective." He draped an arm around the back of her stool.

"Rick is a friend, Thorn, like Josh and Tony."

"That so?" Removing his arm, he watched her, wondering how close she was to Rick Zoeller.

"Yes, it is so. If all you're going to do is pester me, why don't you head out and save us both grief." Shifting away, she did her best to ignore him. Then she felt a slight tug on her ponytail and turned back toward him.

"What do you think of the shop?" He tried to sound indifferent, not wanting Grace to know how much her opinion meant to him.

She could feel the tension radiating from Thorn, wondering if her thoughts truly mattered to him. "You did an incredible job. It's hard to believe you got it all done in such a short time."

"Thanks, Grace. I thought maybe we were pushing too hard. It seemed to work, though. The man you saw me with is Ian Hardesty. He ordered five custom bikes."

Her eyes widened. "That's huge...isn't it?" She had no idea how much profit could be made on one custom job.

He chuckled. "Yeah, it's huge." Finishing his drink, he set the glass on the counter, pursing his lips, deciding whether or not to say what was on his mind. "Have dinner with me."

Grace's lips parted. She hadn't expected the invitation after he'd turned her down for a simple coffee. "I'd like that."

"Good. I know you have a date tonight with the detective, but would Saturday work?"

She flinched, then pushed the unease aside. Rick was a good man, even if he didn't set off a wave of desire the way Thorn did. "Saturday would be perfect."

"All right. I'll pick you up at six." Standing, he started for the door, then glanced over his shoulder. "Dress casual." A broad smile followed, the same one that always caused her heart to race—as it did now.

For a fleeting moment, she wondered if having dinner with him was wise. Whenever she saw him, a small amount of her heart slipped away. The two of them being alone could be a dangerous move, bringing up old memories that could only lead to more regret.

Grace wondered if her desire to spend time with Thorn, learn about his life since leaving town, would be worth the pang of guilt she knew would follow. She felt certain he knew nothing of the pact between her father and his. How would Thorn react when he learned the truth of how they'd both been deceived?

As much as Grace wanted to believe their dinner on Saturday would be a time for understanding, a reconciliation of their friendship, she also worried Thorn learning the truth could push them further apart.

Shaking her head, she took the last sip of her soda, knowing what happened Saturday could very well be too little too late.

Chapter Six

Most times, Grace enjoyed the drive to Buck Springs, a small town half an hour drive from Whiskey Bend. Although surrounded by farms and ranches, the town had become known as a jumping off spot for those seeking adventure in the Bitterroot Mountains. This evening, her thoughts were on Thorn, not her companion in the driver's seat.

Rick Zoeller had picked her up at six, wearing a gray chambray shirt, suede jacket, jeans, and well-worn boots. By any standard, he was a handsome man. Close to six feet tall, his medium brown hair and warm brown eyes drew plenty of attention, including that of the female variety. Why he'd focused his interest on her still puzzled Grace. From all she'd heard, he tended toward curvy blondes with outgoing personalities and a penchant for those in uniform—any uniform, if her information could be trusted.

"Are you all right?"

Grace felt Rick's hand close over hers, and shifted in the bucket seat to look at him. The concern in his eyes moved her. Not for the first time, Grace wished she felt a spark at his touch. After two dates, she already knew their time together wouldn't develop into a serious relationship. She should've refused tonight's invitation, feeling a tinge of guilt at giving him any amount of hope.

Pulling her hand away, she placed it in her lap. "I'm fine. There's been a lot going on and I've had a lot on my mind."

"Care to talk about it over dinner? You look like you could use a drink." Coming to a stop in the restaurant parking lot, Rick shut off the engine.

"A glass of wine does sound wonderful."

He'd called ahead, reserving a table for two overlooking a creek at the back of the property. For such a small town, Buck Springs had one of the finest restaurants in this part of the state. Seeing the table set with a rose and candles, Grace felt another surge of guilt.

"Here you are." Rick pulled out her chair, waiting until Grace sat down, then took a seat across from her. Cozy and round, it would be a miracle if it fit two full-sized plates. "This is one of my favorite restaurants."

"It's lovely, Rick. I've been here a couple times."

He lifted a brow. "Past boyfriends?"

"Afraid not. My father and a few people from work. It's a rare time when he isn't doing something involving Gray Wolf."

"I've heard that about him. It must be hard working with family."

"It can be." Wanting to change the subject, she picked up the menu, taking a minute to make a selection. Resting it on her lap, she waited while the waiter poured wine, took their orders, then walked away. "You've been in Whiskey Bend three years, right?"

"Almost four." Holding up his glass, Rick offered a toast. "To an enjoyable evening."

Touching the rim of her glass to his, Grace took a sip, her gaze wandering to the creek outside. "It's so peaceful here."

He followed her gaze, his expression wistful. "A far cry from where I worked before."

"San Francisco, right?"

Nodding, he rolled the stem of his glass between his fingers, studying the deep red liquid. "Just south of the airport, in one of the wall-to-wall cities stretching forever. I grew up in Los Angeles, so it wasn't much of a change."

"What made you go into law enforcement?"

Chuckling, he took another swallow of wine, then set his glass down. "A bet with my closest friend. We'd both applied to the police academy. Him because he'd wanted to be an officer his whole life, and me because I had nothing else to do. We wagered if one of us didn't make it, he'd owe the other a weekend in the mountains."

"And?"

"We both made it through. He's still a detective south of San Francisco."

"What made you leave?"

A flash of pain crossed his face, his eyes clouding. Grace could see his throat working, although he didn't respond.

"It's all right, Rick. I shouldn't have asked."

Clearing his throat, he swallowed some wine, his fingers clenched around the stem. "I don't talk about it much. It happened about a year before I moved to Whiskey Bend." He looked at her. "It's the reason I came here. My wife and daughter were killed by a drunk driver. He'd already had one DUI, lost his driving privileges for six months, paid a fine—I'm sure you've heard the stories."

"He went to prison, right?"

A bitter laugh escaped his lips. "No. I won't bore you with the legal jargon and loopholes, but as far as I know, he's back out on the streets. I was afraid if I ever ran across him, well...I didn't want to be responsible for what would happen."

The story hit her with such force, Grace couldn't think of anything to say. *I'm sorry* seemed so shallow. Luckily, the waiter appeared with their food, although the eager anticipation of a few minutes before had disappeared.

"May I get either of you anything else?"

Each looked at the waiter and shook their head, neither making a move to pick up their fork.

"I'm sorry, Grace. I didn't mean to talk about this tonight. Fact is, I really don't talk about it at all."

"You've nothing to be sorry about. I can't imagine what you went through, how horrific the entire situation had to have been. I'm honored you shared it with me." A cloud fell over the table, yet she refused to let Rick feel guilty for sharing something so personal. Picking up her fork, she held his gaze. "It smells wonderful."

They ate in silence for a long time before Rick interrupted the quiet. "I'm still pretty screwed up about what happened. It's probably not a good idea for me to be dating, dragging someone into my issues before I've figured them out myself."

She set her fork on the plate, a grim smile on her face. "How about friends?"

Nodding, he seemed to relax. "I'd like that." Sucking in a breath, he seemed to consider his next words. "As a friend, I'd like to ask you something, hoping you don't take it the wrong way."

Her gaze shifted before she brought it back to Rick. "All right."

"How well do you know Thorn Macklin?"

Grace sucked in a quick breath. It was the last thing she'd expected him to ask. "Well, I've known him since we were kids. We were, um...close in high school, then went our separate ways after graduation. Why do you ask?"

"Nothing specific. I'm always curious when anything out of the ordinary happens—like an arson fire."

Her eyes widened. "They've determined it was arson and not bad wiring or some other cause?"

"I got the report before leaving headquarters today. A good percentage of arson fires at a business are started by the owner."

Crossing her arms, Grace's gaze bore into Rick's. "I may not have seen Thorn in several years, but I can assure you he would never start a fire. Not ever."

Holding up his hands, he shook his head. "I'm not accusing him, just trying to understand the people affected. With any crime, knowing who's closest to the incident can provide other clues."

"I can tell you he doesn't need the money. He bought the property and improved the garage using cash. Besides, Scorpion just started, and from what he told me, they already have several orders. He'd have no reason to torch his own place."

Rick chuckled at her wording. "Torch, huh?"

Her irritation dissipated somewhat. Grace didn't even know why she'd been so quick to come to Thorn's defense. Shrugging, she picked up her wine glass, drinking the final sip. "Too much television, I suppose."

Nodding, his brows drew together. "It may just be kids seeing what it felt like to start a fire. Somehow, though..."

"What?"

"I can't give details, but what the arson investigator discovered seems too sophisticated for kids. Regardless, I'm hopeful it was a random incident."

Grace stood at her living room window, looking up at a cloudless sky covered with millions of stars. The house on the edge of town suited her. Two bedrooms and two fireplaces on a large lot with a dozen mature trees, she'd lived here since her return a few years after college. Even with Wolf as her landlord, she found peace in this spot.

She had mixed feelings about her evening with Rick. His decision to stop seeing each other as anything other than friends saved her from doing the same. It was a relief, but she couldn't pull her thoughts from the deal life handed him.

They'd spoken little on the ride back to Whiskey Bend. When they arrived in front of her house, he'd opened her door, escorting her to the porch. She'd thanked him for a wonderful meal. He'd kissed her cheek. All felt right.

Grabbing her purse, she slung it over her shoulder, walking the short distance to her bedroom. Hearing her phone, she rifled through her purse to retrieve it.

"Hello?"

"Hey, it's Thorn."

The familiar ache in her chest didn't surprise her.

"I can call back tomorrow if it's too late."

Even over the phone, she could hear the exhaustion in his voice. "No, this is fine. Did you need to cancel dinner tomorrow night?"

"Not a chance. I wanted to let you know I'll be working at the ranch with Boone and Del all day tomorrow. I may need to pick you up a little later than planned...if that's okay."

She let out a quiet breath. "It's fine. I'll be ready when you get here." Grace tried to think of something witty to say, not wanting to end the call. She could hear music in the background and wondered if he was at home or at Kull's.

"How was your date?"

Sitting on the edge of her bed, Grace couldn't help but think of all the nights during high school when he called after football practice or working on the ranch. They'd talk for so long, either her parents or his would order them to get off.

"It was fine."

"Just fine? I suppose it couldn't have been great if you're already home."

She didn't miss the husky surprise in his voice. "How do you know he isn't here?"

The hesitation told her she'd hit a nerve. "Is he...there with you?"

She enjoyed hearing the uncertainty in his voice. "I wouldn't be talking to you if he were. Rick is a nice guy, Thorn. I'm sure you'll figure that out once you've been in town a while."

"Yeah, maybe. So when's your next date?"

As if it was his business. "If this is going to be twenty questions, I'll let you get back to whatever it is you're doing."

"I'm talking to you, Grace. You're right, though. You don't owe me any explanations on your personal life."

The weariness she heard touched a spot in her heart. She should hang up, let him get on with his night, and get herself to bed. Wolf had called an early meeting in the morning, which meant her Saturday would start at seven and end after noon. As much as she wanted to work in her yard tomorrow, it was good in a strange way. Being in the office wouldn't allow her much time to fret over her evening with Thorn.

"Did you do anything special tonight?" As soon as the words were out, she bit her lip, wishing she'd kept them to herself.

"Not hardly, unless you call a glass of beer, old reruns, and warmed leftover stew special."

Her tension eased a bit, knowing he'd spent his night alone. "If it's any consolation, I spend many nights doing the same. Minus the beer, of course."

"Of course. As I recall, you never were much of a drinker."

"You, Josh, and Tony drank enough to make up for it." She fiddled with the edge of her blouse, wishing they could talk all night, wondering what that said about her feelings for Thorn.

"I'd better let you go. Didn't mean to keep you this long." She could hear the same regret in his voice that she felt.

"It's all right. Thanks for calling, Thorn."

"Goodnight, Grace. Sleep tight."

Her stomach clenched at the familiar words. He'd said the same each night when they were together.

"Is that the best you can do, old man?" Boone directed his question to Thorn, then let out a whoop as he let his rope go, watching it settle over the horns of a young steer. "Now *that's* how it's done, gentlemen."

"He's a cocky sonofabitch." Del sat next to Thorn, both astride their horses in one of the larger pastures.

Thorn had tried to rope the same steer three times, missing each time. He glanced at Del. "I'm rusty. What's your excuse?"

"Who can keep up with Boone when he's out here every day? The kid's a machine."

"Your turn, Del." Boone motioned him over, a broad smile on his face.

"Yep, cocky." Del grinned, then readied the rope before kicking his horse.

Thorn watched, warmth and a sense of peace washing through him. As much as he'd enjoyed his time in Special Forces, he'd missed his brothers. Glancing over his shoulder at the ranch house his parents had built, he wondered if Boone ever got lonely all by himself. He knew both his brothers had no problem finding women to fill their free time, yet neither had ever spoken of someone special. At least not the same type of special he once had with Grace.

A bemused grin tipped up the corners of his mouth when he thought of their conversation on the phone last night. It seemed so much like old times, he had to remind himself fourteen years had passed. He could remember their last call as well as his own name.

They'd graduated a few days before with plans to drive to Missoula on Saturday. He'd listened as Grace listed what she wanted to see and do, thinking they'd never accomplish it all before driving home. Still, the anticipation had been exciting, carrying him through until Saturday morning when he'd arrived at her house.

Wolf had stepped onto the porch, and in his own succinct way, told Thorn she'd left to live with relatives and it was time he made something of himself. The implication had been clear. Wolf didn't believe Thorn was good enough for Grace. At first, he'd stood frozen in place, his mind not comprehending the situation. When Wolf refused to give details of where Grace had gone or how to contact her, he'd stormed off. The subsequent argument with his father had led him to the recruitment office the following day.

"Hey, Thorn. You working or what?" Boone waved, breaking into his thoughts.

"Hell yes, I'm working." Pushing the past behind him, as he did each time the memories claimed his thoughts, he kicked his horse. Maybe he'd get some answers tonight.

Chapter Seven

Grace couldn't sit still. Knowing he'd be a little later than six o'clock, she had changed her plans to be ready whenever he arrived. Almost two hours later, she wondered if he'd reconsidered, or worse, forgotten.

Grabbing her phone, she checked for a text. Nothing. An instant later, it buzzed with a message.

On my way.

She let out a breath, slipping the phone into her purse. Checking in the mirror once again, Grace chided herself for worrying so much about her appearance. He knew what to expect, even been so crass as to remind her, in no uncertain terms, the day he'd shown up at the park. Instead of being angry at the memory, her lips curved into a half-smile. Something about him remembering pleased her.

Hearing the distinct sound of his Harley, her chest tightened, a roar of anticipation ripping through her. It had been years since she'd ridden behind him, hugged his waist as they'd swerved around the winding mountain roads. Glancing down at her old boots, she wondered what he had in mind for tonight. A hard knock had her opening the door, her throat tight as she took in the sight of him leaning against the doorframe in his jeans and leather jacket.

"You're late." The stern tone belied the faint grin and glint in her eyes.

Pushing away, he nodded, walking past her. "Sorry. It took longer to finish Boone's list of things that needed to get done." Coming to a stop a few feet inside, he turned to let his gaze wander over her slowly, obvious appreciation on his face.

"Nice boots." His voice held a husky edge.

"The same ones you bought me."

"Yeah, I remember."

Their eyes held for several seconds, neither moving, his arms hanging loose at his sides. She could see him flex his hands, always a sign he was either tense or angry.

"You ready?"

"Been ready for a while now. Where are we going?" She grabbed her purse, slipping it over her head and across her body, then reached for her old helmet. Gripping her arm, he stopped her.

"Leave it. I have a new one for you to use."

She raised a brow. "Are you wearing one?"

He tilted his head. "Nope."

"Then I'm not wearing one."

"Yes, Grace, you are."

Grace remembered being required to wear one until she turned eighteen. She'd seen Thorn on his bike several times since his return. Not once had he worn a helmet.

"But—"

"Wear a helmet or we take your car. Which will it be?"

They glared at each other a few seconds until she let out an irritated breath. "Fine. I'll wear the helmet."

"Good choice."

A few minutes later, her annoyance vanished as Thorn set them on a path out of Whiskey Bend, toward Missoula. Grace had tolerated the trip with her father a few days ago. Tonight, she couldn't get past the giddy feeling of holding tight against his firm back, the wind whipping past as he navigated one curve after another.

Coming to a stop at an intersection, he made a turn onto a road she'd never noticed. Leaning forward, she spoke as loud as possible against his ear.

"Where are we going?"

He didn't answer. Instead, she felt his strong left hand grip her calf and squeeze, a pang of regret flashing through her. It had always been his signal for her to enjoy the ride and trust him. Strangely enough, she did trust him. The realization should've scared her. Instead, she found herself wondering if he might still harbor feelings for her. If somehow there might still be a chance for them.

Looking ahead, she saw lights. As they got closer, a large log building came into view, a good-sized parking lot to one side. Turning in, Thorn shut off the engine, glancing over his shoulder.

"This is it."

Beautiful and imposing, Grace had never seen the place before. Never even heard of it. A sign above the door announced they'd arrived at Moose Landing.

Climbing off the bike, she removed her helmet, handing it to Thorn after he swung his leg over the seat. "Have you been here before?"

Grace shook her head. "Never. I didn't even know it existed."

"It didn't until about a year ago. An army buddy of mine, plus a few of his friends, started it. Word of mouth only. No advertising. He opens the restaurant Thursday through Saturday nights. The rest of the time he runs a guide service out of Missoula."

She thought of how much work it took to keep a restaurant open. "How does he stay in business?"

Shrugging, he threaded his fingers through hers and started up the steps. "They've been profitable since their third month."

The warmth of his strong, calloused hand sent shivers through her. Grace's mind burned with memories of all the times they'd held hands, aware of the contact, yet not truly appreciating it like she did tonight.

A vivid memory lingered of them sitting together on a bench, watching a stream surge past, her hand in his. They'd been talking of the future. How he wanted to open a motorcycle shop, and she wanted to be a teacher. Once she got her a degree and landed a job in Whiskey Bend, they'd marry. She'd forgotten how much she wanted it. A flash of intense grief tore through her when she thought of the directions their lives had taken. So different from their dreams.

Except Thorn had made changes in his life, focusing on what inspired him all those years ago. Envy coursed through her. In her heart, the thought of teaching still made her pulse quicken. Grace felt as if she'd taken the easy way out by accepting the job her father had dangled in front of her. Better pay than a teacher and infinite possibilities for moving up the corporate ladder.

"Are you all right?"

Glancing up, she realized how far her thoughts had strayed. Looking around, she saw they stood inside a large entry with log beams and a river rock fireplace. A second massive fireplace could be seen in the main dining room.

"Yes, I'm fine." Grace smiled. "Better than fine. This place is magnificent."

Squeezing her hand, he walked up to the hostess stand. "Thorn Macklin. I have a reservation."

An attractive young woman checked her book, then nodded. "Yes, Mr. Macklin. Your table is ready."

Grace tugged his hand. "Is your friend here tonight?"

"No, but he said he'd hook us up."

Following the hostess, she showed them to a table beside the fireplace with a view of the mountains. Floodlights highlighted the area, including what appeared to be a natural spring. Grace found herself glancing at the other diners, wincing at her own worn jeans and scuffed boots. At least her blouse and jacket were presentable.

"Stop worrying. You look great."

"Cut it out."

Chuckling, he pulled out her chair. "What?"

"Reading my mind. It's annoying."

"Then don't be so easy to read."

The hostess stifled a laugh, handing them the menus. "Your waiter will be right over."

"What do you want to drink, Grace? Wine, beer, whiskey?"

"Well, I don't know. What are you having?"

"A soda. I don't drink when I'm on the bike."

"Then I'll have a soda, too." She glanced at the menu, scanning the items. "Have you eaten here before?"

"No. I've come by a couple times to visit, read the menu. That's how I decided to bring you here."

The right corner of her mouth lifted into a smile. "Well, I'm quite impressed."

"You haven't had anything to eat yet. Maybe you'll find it's not quite as impressive as you believe."

Her eyes shifted away, then back to him. "I wasn't talking about this place."

Thorn's gaze sharpened on her, his lips parting. Before he could respond, their waiter appeared.

"May I explain any of the specials?"

He looked across the table at her. "Do you know what you want, Grace?"

Clearing her throat, she dragged her gaze away. "Yes. I'll have the grilled salmon and Caesar salad. I'd prefer no anchovies."

The waiter chuckled. "Few people ask for them. And for you, sir?"

Thorn couldn't stop watching her, his mind still focused on the comment she'd made before the waiter arrived. "The same, please. Except I *will* have the anchovies. And two sodas."

"Yes, sir. Your salads will be right out."

Grace stood, picking up her purse as the waiter walked away. "I'm going to find the ladies' room."

Thorn watched her leave, admiring the tempting sway of her hips, again wondering what she meant about being impressed. The ride from Whiskey Bend tested his self-control. He hadn't been so tempted by the presence of a female in a long time. Grace's arms wrapped around his waist brought back memories better left forgotten. The warmth of her touch almost wiped out the anger he'd held onto each day, through every mission, since she'd left town without a backward glance.

Thorn needed to remember neither of them were naïve teenagers anymore. They were adults, sharing no memories since they were eighteen. He had other lovers over the years, and guessed Grace had, too. Perhaps she'd even fallen in love.

Thanking the waiter when he set down their drinks, he picked his up, touching it to his lips before taking a sip. He'd brought her here to discover if Grace knew more about why her father had turned against him. Thorn never saw it coming. One day, Wolf treated him as a son. The next, he'd cut him off without warning. Thorn wanted to know why.

Grace leaned back against the locked bathroom door. Closing her eyes, she forced herself to breathe—big gulps she hoped would oxygenate her brain, returning some facet of common sense. Her body had been in a state of coiled tension since climbing on the back of the Harley. She didn't understand how such intense heat could pass through two leather jackets, yet it had.

When he got off the bike and took her hand, she wanted to tug him into the bushes and kiss him until they couldn't breathe. Even after fourteen years, her body's reaction to him hadn't changed at all. Neither had her heart.

Covering her face with both hands, she groaned, knowing a decision had to be made. She had two options— let him know how she felt, or accept tonight as a lesson learned and not see him again.

The first caused a cold sweat to form on her forehead. If he didn't feel the same, she'd humiliate herself in front of the one person she truly admired. The second option left a cold ball of ice in her stomach, twisting her heart. What she couldn't do was go on seeing him, pretending she felt nothing but friendship.

Pushing away from the door, she ran some cold water, using one of the disposable hand towels to cool the flush on her face. Staring in the mirror, confusion turned to hope as she thought about the many talks she had with Mr. Weiker, how he'd encouraged her to go after what was in her heart. At eighteen, she'd known exactly what she wanted—a life with Thorn and a teaching job in Whiskey Bend. Neither had worked out for her.

Grace knew she stood at a crossroads. Sucking in a breath, she prepared herself to return to the table, and to Thorn, hoping she had the courage to make a decision on one road or the other.

A familiar tingling filled his stomach as Grace approached. She'd removed the band holding her braid, letting her hair fall over her shoulders. He'd never seen anyone so beautiful. Standing, he pulled out her chair.

"Are you all right?"

Brushing a strand of hair from her face, she nodded, giving him a half-smile. "Yes, I'm fine." She sank into the chair and picked up her soda, sucking in a breath when Thorn's fingers brushed against her neck. Then again when his warm breath brushed over her as he whispered in her ear.

"Are you sure, sweetheart? Because you look tense."

In that instant, her heart seemed to stop beating. She couldn't talk or form a coherent thought.

"Here you are." The waiter approached, carrying their salads, forcing Thorn to return to his seat. "Would either of you like pepper?"

Settling in his chair, a knowing smile lifted his lips, recognizing the confusion on Grace's face. "None for me, thanks."

"Ma'am?"

"Um, no...not for me."

"I know toasting with soda isn't traditional, but..." He shrugged, lifting his glass. "To a renewed friendship, whatever that means."

Ignoring the lump in her throat, she touched her glass to his. "Yes, whatever that means."

Picking up his fork, Thorn took several bites of salad. "Do you feel like talking?"

Her fork stopped midway to her mouth, a leaf of romaine falling to the plate. "Of course. What do you want to talk about?"

He pushed the empty plate aside, leaning his arms on the table. "Why did you leave Whiskey Bend without telling me?"

The fork tumbled from her fingers, salad spilling onto the napkin in her lap. Muttering to herself, Grace returned the food to her plate, licking her lips. Taking a breath, she straightened her spine.

"Father told me we were going to visit relatives. I didn't realize what he meant until we were at the airport. Three suitcases were in the trunk—filled with my clothes. He handed me a ticket across country, telling me it was time I got my head on straight and did something to make him proud." Tears welled in her eyes, but she refused to stop. "When I told him I wouldn't leave without seeing you, he said it was too late. Your father had already sent you away."

Thorn moved his arms from the table and clenched the arms of the chair, his jaw tightening. An icy chill settled over him.

"I wouldn't have left without seeing you, Grace. In fact, I wouldn't have left at all if your father hadn't told me you were already gone." He didn't tell her the rest of what Wolf said, the words that cut Thorn in two.

"How were the salads?" The waiter held plates of grilled salmon and sautéed vegetables.

On auto-pilot, each moved their salad plate aside, making room for their dinner.

"Let me know if I can get you anything else."

Grace stared down at the full plate, her stomach churning. No hunger remained, only a ball of pain.

"You never tried to find me."

Her words cut through him. He'd thought the same many times, wishing he'd tried harder to look for her after graduating from boot camp.

"After learning you were gone, I enlisted in the army. They sent me to Fort Benning, Georgia, with minimal time allowed to contact anyone. I did get a quick call off to Del. He verified you really were gone, but hadn't been able to find out anything more. The call lasted no more than a minute. In reality, I had no way of finding you." His food forgotten, he rested against the back of the chair, lifting his face to the ceiling. "When did you find out your father lied?"

She brushed away a couple stray tears, then took a swallow of soda. "Something about the way it all happened gnawed at me. I couldn't sleep, hardly ate." Her gaze met his. "I was miserable, Thorn. I confronted Father on a trip home from college my sophomore year, told him I'd never come home again if he didn't tell me the truth. It took a bit, but he finally relented. That's when I learned he lied about you leaving. He wanted to separate us, confessing you'd come to the house looking for me and he'd sent you away. He swore he had no idea where you were."

Taking a breath, she watched the fire, regret heavy on her shoulders. "Just before I graduated, I sent a letter to Josh, asking if he knew anything about you. I didn't know he'd enlisted in the navy or Tony had joined the Marines. It took weeks, but Josh's mother wrote back saying you were in the army, stationed somewhere back east. Father and I spoke little over the years. We still barely speak."

His brows furrowed. "But you and Wolf were so close."

"Not after he sent me away and confessed to lying. He betrayed both of us, Thorn. I don't know if I'll ever be able to put it behind me."

Pushing back his chair, Thorn stood, pulling out some big bills and throwing them on the table. He held out his hand, his face full of determination. "Let's get out of here."

Standing, she threaded her fingers through his. "Where are we going?"

"Someplace where we can figure this whole thing out."

Chapter Eight

Dropping Grace's hand as they approached the Harley, Thorn pulled out his phone, sending a quick text. Neither spoke as she tightened her helmet, then settled herself behind him. She didn't know or care where they were headed.

Thorn took the highway back to Whiskey Bend, turning onto a well-packed dirt road several miles from town. Grace already felt better. Something about being on the back of the bike, the wind blowing across her face, the scenery feeling close enough to touch, always calmed her. Having her arms wrapped around Thorn didn't hurt.

Looking over his shoulder, she saw a rustic cabin in a clearing, lighted only by the moon overhead. As they got closer, she saw it had one story with a wraparound porch and stone chimney. She loved it.

Pulling to a stop a few feet from the steps, they climbed off. Taking her hand, he led her up the steps, grabbed a key from a hiding place, and opened the door.

"Is this your place?"

"No. It belongs to Del. He comes up here on his days off or when he needs to get away. I sent him a text saying I planned to use it tonight."

Her stomach flipped at his words and their implication. "All night?" She couldn't help the slight squeak in her voice.

He stopped his search for something to drink and looked at her, his expression bland. "Nothing's going to happen tonight, Grace, other than talk." The corners of his mouth twitched, as if he were suppressing a smile. Stalking toward her, he stopped inches away and leaned down, his eyes dark and searching. "Of course, if you'd rather talk tomorrow..."

Placing her hands on his chest, she pushed him away, her heart almost bursting. "Talking would be best." She didn't believe it, but knew they had a lot of gaps to fill.

"Good idea." Stepping around her, he bent down by the fireplace, arranging kindling and a couple lightweight logs.

Grace did her best to hide the disappointment at how easily he'd agreed. A part of her hoped he'd wrap his arms around her, kiss her the way he used to, leaving her breathless and needy.

He glanced over his shoulder. "There's soda, water, beer, and wine in the refrigerator. Grab what you want."

"Water sounds good. What would you like?"

"The same. I think it will be best to keep a clear head tonight." Satisfied with the initial flames, Thorn piled more logs on the fire, then stood, brushing his hands down his jeans. Taking the bottle she offered, he gestured toward the sofa. "Have a seat."

She sat down on one end of the sofa, while he chose a chair across from her. It already took all his willpower not to drag her into his arms and do what he'd dreamed of for fourteen years. Being too close would test him beyond his limits.

Leaning back, he rested his right ankle on his left thigh and took a long swallow of water. Even from this distance, he could feel tension radiating from her, see the slight shake of her hands. He'd taken plenty of prisoners, witnessed the telltale signs of fear, and felt a stab of guilt. Hauling her onto his lap, stroking away any discomfort, would solve one problem, but open a whole bundle of others.

"I don't want you to feel trapped, Grace. I'll take you back to your place if you're uncomfortable."

She shook her head. "No. I'd rather stay where we're certain of privacy. We need to get this all out."

"It could take all night."

"I know, but I think we owe it to ourselves to learn the truth, don't you?" She searched his face, knowing he wanted the same.

"Yes, I do." Sucking in a breath, he cocked his head to one side. "Where to start..."

She shifted, tucking her legs underneath her. "Well, you already know I went to college. I worked near campus a couple years, then Father offered me a job back here. That's it. Pretty boring."

"What happened to your dream of being a teacher?" He saw regret wash across her face, then quickly vanish.

"It must not have been as important as I once believed." She looked down, fidgeting with the edge of her jacket.

"You can take that off if you're too hot."

She glanced up. "What?"

"The leather jacket. It's starting to warm up in here. I can hang it by the door for you."

Grace did feel a bit warm. She slid out of it, handing it to him. "Thanks."

He also took his off, hanging it beside hers, then checked the fire before sitting back down.

"Tell me about you, Thorn. All I know is you were in the Special Forces."

He shrugged, staring down at his hands. "Not much to tell. I enlisted, got through boot camp, was identified for advanced training, and before I knew it, qualified for Special Forces."

"You're being modest. From what I've heard, only the army's best make it that far."

Thorn winced. There were a lot of good men and women in the various fields in the army, all contributing their talent. His were just one part of what made up the military.

"I did travel a bit."

"Where?"

"Some places you'd expect, some you might not. Primarily the Middle East, a little time in Africa. Made some lifelong friends." He thought of his team, knowing a couple would be getting out soon, possibly joining him in Whiskey Bend.

She glanced at his ring finger, already knowing it was bare. "You never married."

His gaze traveled over her, desire and longing filling him until he couldn't sit a moment longer. Standing, he walked over to the fire. "No, I never married. You?"

"No."

"Ever get close?"

Her heart squeezed at how close she'd come, then lost him. "Just once."

All the same feelings he'd bottled up inside showed on her face. The same need, same regret, same pain. Without thought, his feet moved. Before he knew it, he'd settled beside her, placing an arm around her shoulders. Pulling her close, he kissed her temple, then rested his chin on the top of her head.

"I've missed you so damn much, Grace." He breathed the words against her hair, feeling shivers ripple through her. "I haven't been a saint all these years. Far from it. But you were always who I wanted. You're the only woman I've ever loved."

She buried her face in her hands, her body shaking as the tears came. "I'm sorry. I never cry. Never. This is all so much."

He tightened his hold, needing to do whatever he could to relieve her pain. "I know you probably don't feel the same. Hell, you're dating, enjoying life, then I show up, dredging up all kinds of unwanted memories." He drew in a ragged breath. "Come on. I'll take you home."

"No." She looked up at him, her eyes pleading. "Please. I want to stay."

He couldn't pull his gaze from hers. "Grace, I..."

Placing a finger over his mouth, she leaned up, brushing her lips against his. The one touch was all it took to ignite all the years of waiting and wanting.

"Grace, this may not be a good idea."

Her eyes warmed as she touched her lips to his again. This time, he didn't object, his mouth settling over hers for a deep kiss that continued until they were both breathless. Pulling away, he lifted her onto his lap.

"Ah, Grace. I've never been able to say no to you."

Wrapping her arms around his neck, she drew him back down, unable to stop what they'd started.

Chuckling against her mouth, he lifted his head, his face darkening. "You need to know I'm not playing around here, Grace. I want to try again, see if we can make it work. If you aren't sure or need more time, we should cool this off, wait until each of us is certain."

His words shot through her, reminding Grace she had responsibilities, a life she'd built without him. She hadn't told Thorn about the new position in Austin. Her father would demand a decision this week, and she still had no idea what to tell him.

She could turn it down and hope it all worked out with Thorn. But what if it didn't? What if, after a few weeks or months, they realized they couldn't get back what they'd once had?

Dropping her arms from around his neck, she shifted off his lap to sit beside him.

"I've never loved anyone else. So, yes, I'd like to try again, but you're right. We need to be certain before doing anything that could cause either of us more pain." She swallowed, quelling the rampant desire that ruled her a few moments before. "If we could take it slow..." She glanced up at him, seeing a grin spread across his face.

"Sweetheart, we can take it as slow as you want. All I'm asking for is a chance." Leaning down, he placed one more quick kiss across her lips, then stood. "I'm exhausted. Let's get some rest. Tomorrow, we'll sort this out."

Her brow lifted. "How many beds?"

"One. You can trust me, Grace. We'll hold each, nothing more. Is that all right?"

Taking his outstretched hand, she stood. "I trust you, Thorn. I've always trusted you."

Grace had never woken with a man's arms wrapped around her. In high school, they'd never been able to find more than a few hours alone. Afterward, she'd never wanted to spend the night with the two men she'd been somewhat serious about. She wanted her private space, a bed without the memories of another man infringing. This morning, her feelings were different. So much so, she had no desire to move from Thorn's strong embrace.

He'd done what he said, doing nothing except holding her while she slept. Although rested, disappointment rushed through her. Grace knew he was right. They had a lot to work out. Although making love with Thorn would be wonderful, it would cloud the issues, making rational decisions difficult.

"You think too much. We'll work this all out." He nuzzled her neck, trailing kisses along her shoulder.

His rough, husky voice and warm lips felt wonderful against her sensitive skin.

"How do you know?"

"Hmmm..."

She tried to think, finding it difficult when he pulled back her hair, sucking the sensitive spot below her ear. "How do you know it will all work out?"

Placing one more kiss on her shoulder, he settled back on the pillow. "Because I've always believed you and I were meant to be together." He sat up, pulling her with him until she rested against his side. "When I came home and found out you were still single, I felt hope for the first time in years."

"Aren't you scared?" She shook her head, her hand resting on the t-shirt covering his chest. "Of course you aren't. Nothing scares you."

"Hell yeah, I get scared. Every time my team went out to face the enemy, my stomach churned. Seeing you for the first time in years almost knocked me on my butt."

She glanced up at him, her eyes wide. "It did?"

"Scout's honor. That's why I refused to meet you for coffee. I wasn't ready for a one-on-one with you."

"It's hard for me to believe I could scare you so much."

Chuckling, he rested his chin on the top of her head. "Sweetheart, you scare me more than the fiercest enemy overseas. I know how to get the best of him. With you, well...I'm not on solid ground."

She couldn't hide the smile spreading across her face as she touched the tight muscles of his chest. "You feel pretty solid to me."

Squeezing her one more time, he set her aside, getting out of the bed.

Sitting up, she watched him bend over to grab his boots, admiring the way he filled out his jeans. "I can't believe we wore all our clothes to bed."

"Trust me, sweetheart, it was the only way we wouldn't do what both of us wanted." Running fingers through his hair, he turned back to her, his gaze narrowing. "You're a huge temptation, Grace, but I want to get this right. There's too much at stake to mess it up."

Her heart squeezed at his honesty. "I feel the same."

"With both of us having the same goal, I don't see how we can lose."

As much as Grace wanted to agree, she couldn't ignore the warning bells in her head. She'd given serious thought to her father's offer, finding few reasons to turn it down. Now she had an excellent one. Declining the promotion wouldn't be easy, knowing Wolf would press her for the reason. Thorn could not be her answer.

Grace didn't know if she could trust Wolf to stay out of her business, letting the relationship with Thorn develop on its own. He'd betrayed her once before. She couldn't allow herself to believe he'd leave them alone this time.

Thorn's hand on her shoulder drew her thoughts back to him. Looking up, she saw the corners of his mouth curving down with concern.

"You're not still worried about us, are you?" He bent down, kissing her forehead.

She shook her head. "No, not about our feelings for each other."

Sitting on the bed next to her, Thorn pulled her close. "Then what?"

Drawing in a deep breath, she tucked closer into his side. "Father offered me a promotion."

"Is that a problem?"

"It is when it's located in Texas."

Chapter Nine

Thorn stood under the shower, letting the hot spray sluice down his body, helping to clear his head. He'd kept silent as Grace explained the opportunity in Austin, his gut clenching the more he learned. It would be her chance to show the board, and everyone else, what she could do, giving her a real chance at taking over when Wolf retired.

After asking a few questions, he'd invited her to join him in the shower, needing to feel her body against his. She declined. It had been a wise choice. Grabbing the bottle of shampoo, he lathered his head, massaging the liquid into his scalp. Another action meant to clear his head, help him come to terms with all that had happened.

He didn't want to lose Grace, but he'd never stand in her way. Thorn knew what it was like to have a dream and the chance to achieve it. Offering her anything less would be selfish.

"Coffee?"

Poking his head out of the shower, his face brightened at the sight of Grace holding out a cup.

"You still take it black?" She leaned against the closed door, cradling her own cup in both hands.

"Nothing but." Taking a sip, he set the cup on the vanity, then slipped back under the warm spray of the shower.

"Can I make you breakfast? I found eggs, bacon, and a loaf of bread. It wouldn't take long."

His stomach growled, but the thought of food didn't appeal to him. "You go ahead. I'll be out in a few minutes."

Waiting until he heard the door open and close, he turned off the water. Drying off, he wrapped the towel around his waist, then placed his hands on the vanity.

He stared into the sink, then raised his head to study his reflection in the mirror. The same face stared back at him. The one he saw every day. After holding Grace all night, he'd hoped to see something different. The explanation of her job offer flipped his thinking.

Thorn slipped into the same clothes as the night before, then headed to the kitchen, determined to do what was best for Grace.

"I know you said for me to go ahead, but it's just as easy to cook for two as one." She handed him a plate with four eggs, over easy, bacon, and toast.

"You remembered." A grin brightened his face.

"Yeah. Black coffee and runny eggs. Some things don't change."

He grabbed the fork and knife she held out, taking a seat at the table. "You going to join me?"

A slight grin crossed her face as she set her plate down and took a seat next to him.

Waiting until she scooped up some eggs, Thorn dug into his. "These are great," he mumbled, washing the food down with coffee.

Neither spoke as they finished breakfast. Grace pushed her chair back, reaching for his empty plate when Thorn gripped her arm.

"Sit down. I have something to say."

A sick, empty feeling erupted in the pit of her stomach. The combination of regret and determination on his face did nothing to alleviate her fears.

He swallowed the lump in his throat, managing a thin smile. "I think you should take it."

She blinked a couple times, her lips parting. "Take it?"

"The job in Austin. You've worked hard and have a chance to prove what you can do on a higher level. From what I've heard, it's a great place for upwardly mobile people like you."

Her heart sank. "Upwardly mobile?"

"Sure." He drained the last of his coffee, setting the cup down. "You're an achiever, Grace. Austin is the place to show off your skills. Besides, the money sounds great. You'll be able to get that sports car you always talked about."

"How do you know I don't already own it?" Her heart ached too much to say more. Desperate for space, she stood, grabbing the dirty plates.

"Grace..."

Setting the dishes in the sink, she started the water and closed her eyes, trying to calm the growing ache in her chest. She heard the sound of his chair grating on the worn wooden floor, tried to ignore his arms wrapping around her from behind, drawing her to his chest.

"Grace..." His warm breath brushed across her cheek before he placed a kiss on her neck. "You know it's what you want."

She wanted to scream. It wasn't what she wanted. Had never been what she wanted. Those choices had been taken from her years ago because of a pact between two controlling fathers.

"What do you know about what I want?" Pushing away from the sink, she spun around, her cheeks flushed. "I'm sure you have work to do, and I need to get back home."

Before he could react, she stormed down the hall and into the bedroom, returning seconds later with her purse over her shoulder. She didn't get far.

Thorn blocked the front door, refusing to budge when she tried to skirt around him. Placing his hands on her shoulders, he waited until she settled down.

"If I don't know what you want, it's because you haven't shared it with me. Talk to me, Grace. Help me understand what's important to you."

As much as she wanted to argue, Thorn was right. She hadn't ever spoken of her desire to leave Gray Wolf, get out from under her father's thumb. The fact he knew of her job search didn't impact her decision on the promotion. Accepting it would get her hundreds of miles away from his daily scrutiny, allowing her to think through her future without pressure. Her quiet, unassuming mother would never contradict her husband or offer Grace guidance. She never had.

Until Thorn returned, she'd forgotten about her love of teaching. It now sat on the edges of her consciousness, a younger, idealistic version of Grace encouraging her to follow her heart. She wanted to confide in Thorn, tell him of the desire she'd buried for years, yet fear of expressing her true thoughts tightened her throat.

His urging her to accept the promotion had been a surprise after he admitted she was the only woman he ever loved. She'd taken it to mean he still loved her. Perhaps she'd misunderstood, and encouraging her to take the opportunity in Austin was his way of gaining distance.

Shaking her head, Grace moved out of his hold. There were too many mixed signals to sort through right now. She didn't want to make another mistake.

"A lot has happened since you picked me up last night. Perhaps it's best to take a few days, think about what we both want."

Letting out a deep breath, he nodded. Thorn couldn't make her stay and bare her soul. After all, he'd been the one to encourage her to take the promotion. Her reaction clearly showed he'd made a mistake. She'd asked for time. He would give her as much as she needed.

"I'll get the bike ready."

Watching him walk outside, she crossed her arms, a cold chill washing over her. She'd been right to ask for a few days, time to sort through her thoughts and choices. Then why did she feel the biggest opportunity of her life was in the form of a tall man with broad shoulders and a wicked smile?

Setting the wrench aside, Thorn scrubbed a hand down his face. The day hadn't gone as he'd hoped.

Until Grace had asked for some space, he'd envisioned them spending the day together, maybe taking a long motorcycle ride. Instead, he'd dropped her off at home, then rode straight to the shop. Working calmed his nerves, gave him something to focus on other than the doubts piling up. The promotion threw a whole new set of obstacles in their path, but he'd be damned if he would stand in the way of Grace achieving her goals.

Tony ambled in, clothes and hair ruffled. "Didn't expect to see you here today, boss."

Thorn shook his head. "Geez, man. You look like you just got out of bed."

A broad smile spread across Tony's face. "And a very nice bed it was."

Chuckling, Thorn picked the wrench back up. "Do I know her?"

"Probably, but you won't hear her name from me."

"Understood. What brings you in on a Sunday?"

"Thought I'd review the drafts Josh prepared for the bikes Ian Hardesty ordered. We have a good timeframe, but I'd still like to order materials as soon as possible." Tony rubbed his eyes with the palms of his hands.

Thorn failed to contain a smirk. "You sure you don't want to sack out on the cot in back?"

"What? Nah, I'm fine." Stretching his arms above his head, he glanced at the bike Thorn worked on. "A Sportster, huh? I don't recognize it."

"I bought it off a local rancher a couple weeks ago. It belonged to his son." Thorn glanced at Tony when he crouched down next to him. "He died in Afghanistan."

Tony blew out a breath. "Rough."

"Yeah. Anyway, the rancher sold it to me for almost nothing." Thorn ran his hand over the leather seat.

Tony rubbed the back of his neck. "If memory serves, didn't Grace talk about getting a Sportster when we were in high school?"

He'd hoped his friend wouldn't recall the way she'd dragged them around looking for a used bike after they offered to fix it up for her. When Wolf discovered what they were doing, he put a quick stop to it.

Thorn shrugged. "Could be."

Tony didn't believe there wasn't a plan for the bike. "So you bought one, are fixing it up, and will give it to...who?"

"No one, all right? I got it for a good price. Thought we could trick it out and put it in the showroom. You okay with that?"

Tony stood, holding up his hands. "Hey, no problem, man." He took one more look at the bike, then turned to leave. "I'll be on the computer if you need me."

Thorn let out a breath, unable to take his eyes off the slick Harley Grace had wanted. Tony caught on right away. He *had* bought it with her in mind, searching for a way to cut the tension between them. When he'd handed the rancher cash two weeks ago, he didn't have a firm plan—just knew he had to have it. As he held her last night, snuggling as they'd never been able to do as teenagers, his thoughts kept returning to the bike. Fixing it had taken on a sense of urgency.

Even though this morning hadn't gone as he'd hoped, Thorn vowed to trick it out and give it to her prior to her move. He'd teach her to ride, getting her ready to pass the license exam. Maybe they'd have a chance to go for a ride together before she left.

Grim satisfaction shot through him, picturing her face when she saw it. Wolf could no longer forbid her from accepting the gift, and he couldn't prevent her from taking it to Texas.

Before he knew it, two hours had passed. He'd made a good deal of progress, but he had to pick up the pace.

"You interested in taking a break?" Tony asked as he walked up to him.

Standing, Thorn twisted from one side to the other, then stretched out his arms. "Sure. What do you have in mind?"

"It's been a long time since I've been to the range. You up for a friendly competition? Whoever loses buys dinner tonight."

"Absolutely. You want to call Josh, see if he's interested?"

"I'm on it." Tony pulled out his phone, punching in numbers. A minute later, he ended the call. "Josh is in. He'll meet us at the range."

Thorn grinned. "Great. I can't think of a better way to end a weekend than having you two fork over money for my dinner."

"I'm sorry, Mother, but I wouldn't be good company tonight." Grace paced back and forth on her front porch, the phone to her ear.

"Your father would very much like you here, Grace. I don't see why you can't make it."

"I already have plans for dinner, Mother." She glanced through the front window toward her kitchen where a chicken thawed in the sink. "How about next weekend, or some evening this week?"

"Well, maybe. Your father will be very disappointed. We invited our new neighbor. I'm sure you two will hit it off."

Closing her eyes, Grace willed herself to stay calm. Her mother had mentioned the new neighbor several times since he moved in a month ago. Charming, good-looking, and single, if she remembered her description correctly.

"Mother, did Father mention I may be moving to Austin?"

"Well, yes, he mentioned something about it. That's one reason I wanted you to meet him."

Shaking her head, Grace lowered herself onto one of the Adirondack chairs scattered around her porch, breathing out a frustrated sigh, followed by a rush of disappointment. She'd hoped her mother would voice even a slight amount of distress over her leaving, perhaps admit she'd miss her when she left.

If I leave, Grace reminded herself.

Since Thorn had brought her home, she'd struggled with one major issue—his encouragement to take the job. Before last night, her decision had been ninety percent complete. Waking in his arms had pushed the percentage way down, giving her a new sense of purpose and direction. Then he'd voiced his enthusiasm for her leaving. It didn't match how he'd treated her or what he'd said before learning of Wolf's offer. Why the change?

"I'm sorry, Mother, but I can't make it tonight. I'd better let you go so you can get ready for your company."

"There's plenty if you change your mind."

"Good to know. Love you, Mother."

"Love you, too."

Pushing herself up, she shook her head. They said the same words at the end of every call, almost without thought, as if they took it for granted.

Sliding the phone into her pocket, Grace walked inside and straight into the kitchen. She had no idea what to do with the chicken. It always seemed to be her go-to food when she didn't have much of an appetite or needed to keep herself busy. Tonight, it fell into both categories.

Dragging the package onto the counter, she stared at it, having no interest in cooking or eating. Five minutes later, she put it away in the refrigerator, grabbed her car keys, and took off. She had no idea where she was headed. Evie's Diner didn't appeal to her—too many people she knew hung out there on Sunday evenings. Kull's Wicked Waters wouldn't do tonight. Besides, there would be a good chance of running into Thorn if she went there, and she wasn't ready to see him again. Not yet.

If she stuck with local, casual, and affordable, that left Doc's Grill and Tavern. A slow smile lifted her lips when she thought of Diego "Doc" Martinez. When he left the army, the former medic came straight to Whiskey Bend, opened his restaurant, and vowed to never again tend the wounded or dying. He'd carved out a good niche, selling large portions of home-style food and a healthy dose of friendly good humor. She headed straight for it.

Stepping inside, she smelled the rich aroma of his specials—meatloaf, pot roast, lasagna, and the most incredible chicken enchilada casserole this side of the Mississippi.

"Gracie Jackson. Haven't seen you in here in...what? At least a month. That's weeks too long." Doc walked up to her, his arms already outstretched, pulling her into a hug.

"Hi, Doc." She stepped out of his embrace, glancing at his well-used apron. "I see you've been cooking again. Didn't you hire someone to take over for you?"

A frown creased his forehead. "Yeah. Had to fire him. He couldn't get past the fact we're a family grill." Settling his hands on his waist, he shook his head. "Insisted I add all these frou-frou dishes to the menu. Can you imagine how smoked and dried eel or candied beetroot would go over in Whiskey Bend?"

Laughing, she touched his arm. "I think you made a good choice. So you're back in the kitchen full-time?"

"For now. I've got some ideas of who to bring in. A Missoula kid with a great attitude and understanding of what people out here want." He took her arm, walking her to a small table outside the kitchen. "You sit right here. I know exactly what to bring you."

Settling into a chair, she couldn't help the smile on her face. It had been too long since she'd come in.

"Here you are." Doc set a glass of wine in front her. "Malbec. The one good item the previous cook added to the menu. I think you'll like it."

"You know I'll drink about any red wine." Taking a sip, her brows lifted. "You're right. It's great."

"Here's the salad you wanted, Doc."

He took the plate from one of the servers, placing it in front of Grace. "Caesar."

"How did you know that's what I planned to order?"

"Gracie, how long have you been coming in here?"

"Got it. So am I getting the lasagna?"

114

"Nope. I have a better choice for you tonight. It'll be right out."

Smiling, she took another sip of wine, enjoying the rich flavor. Taking a deep breath, she relaxed against the back of the chair, closing her eyes. This was what she needed. A few hours to relax in a place she felt welcome and safe. Opening her eyes, her smile vanished.

Thorn's large frame filled the doorway, his gaze moving over the crowd, then locking on her.

Chapter Ten

Grace's heart pounded and hand shook as she set the wine glass on the table, seeing a slow smile appear on Thorn's face as he made his way to her. Resting a hand on the back of the chair across from her, he took another look around, then turned his attention back to Grace.

"Do you mind if I join you? That is, if you're not meeting someone else."

Her insides churned at how good he looked, fighting the impulse to stand and wrap her arms around his neck. Clearing her throat, she shook her head. "No."

A brow lifted as he cocked his head. "No?"

"I'm mean...no, I'm not meeting anyone. Please, sit down."

Before Thorn could say another word, a waitress appeared, a glass of wine in her hand. "Doc asked me to give this to you." She nodded at Grace. "It's the same as she's drinking."

Although not what he would've ordered, he smiled at the young woman. "Thank you."

"I'll give you some time to check the menu." She started to turn away.

"Please bring me whatever the lady ordered."

"Yes, sir. I'll bring your salad right out."

Holding the glass to his face, he kept his gaze on Grace as he inhaled. "What is it?"

"Doc called it a Malbec. It's very good."

Thorn took a sip, his eyes lighting up. "You're right. It is good." Setting the glass down, he relaxed in his chair, enjoying the view before him. He hadn't expected to see Grace for several days, but now that he had, he meant to make the most of it.

The waitress walked up with his salad. "Here you are. Both your dinners will be ready in a few minutes."

"Thanks." He picked up his fork, looking at Grace.

"Please, go ahead, Thorn. I've already eaten mine."

Digging in, he made short work of the romaine, parmesan, and croutons before pushing the empty plate aside. "What did you do today?"

Shrugging, she tried to calm the way her body responded to him being so close and looking so good. "Worked in the yard a bit, did laundry. You know, all the mundane stuff I don't get done during the week. Did you make it to the shop?"

"For a while. Worked on an old bike I'm restoring." His eyes glistened, hoping Grace would be the one to ride it. "Tony came by for a while. He ended up calling Josh, and the three of us went to the gun range."

Grace thought of the handgun she had in her dresser drawer. She hadn't shot it in months. "I can't remember the last time I was there. How'd you do?" It sounded silly to ask. Everyone knew he was an expert shot.

"I'm better with a rifle, but I did respectable. Outshot Tony and Josh, which is all I cared about. They were supposed to buy me dinner, but Tony got a call from his mother about some emergency at the ranch, and Josh had plans with some woman he met at Evie's. So here I am."

A knowing look flashed across her face. "I'm sure you'll find a way to collect the dinner they owe you."

"From where I'm sitting, this is much better than eating with them." He picked up his glass, tipped it toward her, then took another sip. Setting the glass down, he leaned forward. "You certain you're okay with me being here? I know you wanted some space."

Shifting in her chair, Grace wished they were eighteen again. Life seemed easier, uncluttered, without the layers of decisions inherent in becoming an adult. They'd wake up, go to school, spend time together, then return to their own homes. So much had happened in fourteen years, yet one thing hadn't changed. She still loved Thorn with all her heart.

"I'm fine. It's better than the two of us sitting alone, sneaking glances at each other across the restaurant." She brushed a strand of hair away from her face, humor glistening in her eyes.

He grinned, remembering how they used to do the same in high school. "I suppose you're right."

The waitress walked up, a plate in each hand. "This is a new pasta dish Doc is thinking of adding to the menu. He says dinner is on the house tonight, as long as you give him your honest opinion before you leave."

"Sounds like a deal I can't pass up." Grace picked up her fork and took a bite. "Oh my...it's yummy." Glancing at Thorn, she saw him smirk. "What?"

"Just enjoying how much you appreciate your food." Filling his own fork, he chewed slowly, understanding her reaction. "You're right. This is great. The sauce is as good as the stuffed ravioli."

He continued until he finished every bit, not noticing Grace watching him. Glancing up, his movements stilled when he caught her staring, her expression somber. "You all right?"

Grace continued to study him, not bothering to respond.

"Grace?" When she didn't answer this time, Thorn stood, kneeling down next to her chair. "Are you feeling all right?" He saw the unmistakable look of determination on her face, mixed with something else he couldn't quite define. Before he could comment again, she stood, holding out her hand.

"Take me home, Thorn."

Standing, he grasped her hand, studying her features for a moment. "Sure. I can drive your car and come back for the bike."

Grace shook her head. "No. I want you to take me to *your* home."

His face clouded at an offer he didn't want to refuse. "Do you think that's such a good idea?"

Biting her lower lip, she pierced him with a hard gaze. "I believe it's the best idea I've had in a very long time. Of course, if you don't want me..."

Tightening his grip, he nodded, clearing his throat. "Let's get out of here."

Thorn couldn't get to his place fast enough. He'd thought about her all day while fixing the bike and shooting at the range. Finding her at Doc's had been a nice surprise. Allowing him to join her was a bonus. Asking him to take her home made him feel like he'd won the lottery.

Parking in front of his house, he reached over, grabbing her hand. "Are you sure about this, Grace? We could go inside and have a drink, talk about what's going on inside that beautiful head of yours." He touched a finger to her forehead.

Her eyes darkened, a determined smile tilting up the corners of her mouth. "I'm certain, although I wouldn't turn down a drink."

"Come on." Walking around the car, he opened the door, taking her hand. A moment later, they stood on his porch as he unlocked the door and drew her inside.

He didn't resist when she wrapped her arms around his neck, pulling him down, kissing him with burning intensity. Cupping her face in his hands, he allowed passion to take control as he deepened the kiss, hearing a soft moan escape her lips.

"Grace..." His mouth brushed against hers when he spoke. Breaking the kiss, his lips trailed a path to the pulsing hollow at the base of her throat, his hands splayed across her back, drawing her close. Reclaiming her lips, he crushed her to him, moving his hands to settle on her hips, feeling her return his kiss with a hunger better than anything he could've ever imagined.

Even aligning her body against his didn't get him close enough. With a growl, he broke the kiss, lifting her into his arms, taking long strides to the bedroom. Easing her down on the center of the bed, he gazed at her, his heart swelling as intense emotion ripped through him.

Raising her arms toward him, a sweet smile curved her lips, her glazed eyes searching his. "Thorn, please..."

He'd never been able to deny her anything, and he wouldn't start now. If his team members knew how far their leader had fallen, he'd never hear of the end of it. Years as a Special Forces soldier, yet he turned to goo around her. "You're certain, Grace?"

In response, she began unbuttoning her blouse, letting it fall open, before moving her hands to the button of her jeans.

His jaw tightened, throat thickening as he followed her movements. Bending, he stilled her hands, his voice husky with need. "Let me do that." Stretching out beside her, he took her in his arms once again. "I love you, Grace."

Reaching up, she drew a finger down his cheek, brushing it lightly across his lower lip. "I love you, too, Thorn."

With two important meetings the following morning and the deadline on the promotion a few days away, Grace hadn't meant to stay late. After two rounds of intense lovemaking and Thorn's protective arms wrapped around her, she'd fallen into a deep sleep, waking to the sound of a phone. Groaning, she slipped out of his grasp, tugged the covers down, and reached for her clothes.

"Shhh. It's mine, sweetheart." Thorn's warm breath fanned her neck, sending shivers down her spine. Snaking his arm back around her, he reached behind him.

"Macklin."

"It's Josh. There's another fire at the shop. You'd better get down here."

Thorn uttered a muffled curse. "On my way." He checked the time—almost four in the morning.

"What is it?" Grace turned toward him.

Leaning down, he kissed her lips, then rolled out of bed. "That was Josh. There's another fire."

The news had her fully awake and moving. In less than two minutes they were outside, climbing into her car, and hurrying through the darkness. Three blocks from the shop, Thorn smelled smoke, then saw the glow from the fire. Screeching to a stop half a block away, he bounded from the car.

"Stay here, Grace. I need to find out what happened."

Running up, a police officer stopped him as he tried to jump over the barricade. "Sorry, sir. You can't go any closer."

"It's my shop."

The officer held his hand up. "All the same, my orders are to keep everyone back."

"But—"

"Thorn. Over here." Josh stood outside the barriers about twenty feet away, Tony and Detective Zoeller by his side. On instinct, he glanced behind him toward the car, seeing Grace standing on the sidewalk. Another discussion he'd meant to have with her, which would now have to wait.

Jogging toward them, Thorn stopped when Wolf intercepted him, the man's features hard as stone.

"Where's Grace?"

Thorn motioned behind him. "Waiting by her car." He started to walk away, feeling a hand grip his arm.

"Where was she last night?"

Glaring at Wolf, he shook off his hold. "Not that it's your business, but she was with me. And don't even think about giving her any grief over it. We're together, Wolf, and you'd do well to stay out of it this time." Without waiting for a response, he closed the short distance to the others, his gaze riveted on the flames. "What happened?"

Josh shook his head. "We don't know yet. I got another call, like the first one. By the time I got here, they were already working to control the fire. The couple

123

firefighters I heard talking said something about it starting in the fabrication area. They could be wrong."

"The showroom."

Josh shook his head. "I don't know. They won't let us close enough to get a look."

"The fire's at least three times the size of the last one." This came from Tony, who stood on Thorn's other side.

"Yeah, I can see that." His stomach clenched, thinking of the finished choppers in the showroom, the drawings for Ian, and the Harley for Grace. Insurance would cover the damage, and they'd backed up everything offsite. Still, it would take weeks to get it all back up and running. He hoped Ian wouldn't back out, requesting the return of his deposit.

"Macklin."

Thorn glanced over his shoulder to see Rick Zoeller behind him, his face a mask. "Detective. You got here quick."

Shrugging, he nodded toward a building down the street. "I have an apartment a block away. Heard the sirens."

Turning fully toward Rick, Thorn's jaw hardened. He didn't know the guy, but already didn't like him. He assured himself it had nothing to do with Grace. "Did you get here in time to see anyone?"

"Such as?" Rick smirked.

"Who might have started this. That would be really helpful right now."

"I thought you might be able to shed some light on it. After all, it was your shop."

Thorn turned his back to Zoeller, feeling the heat from the fire rush past him. "It's *still* my shop, Detective. No matter how this turns out, we will rebuild and start again." He couldn't see Rick purse his lips, nodding.

"Figured as much. Look, I want to find whoever did this as much as you, but I have to check off a few boxes first."

This got Thorn's attention. "What boxes?"

"It would be helpful if you and your partners told me where you were tonight. I'd like to eliminate the three of you as soon as possible."

"Look, Zoeller—"

"It's all right, Thorn." Josh looked at Rick. "I was with a girl I'm seeing. I'll be glad to give you her name...in private."

"And you?" Rick looked at Tony.

"Closed the bar at Wicked Waters. Kull didn't want me to drive, so he gave me a cot to sack out on. Woke up when I heard the fire engines."

Rick looked at Thorn. "And you?"

"At home, asleep."

"Alone?"

He clamped his mouth shut, his gaze fixed on the detective.

"He was with me, Rick."

Thorn mumbled a curse, seeing Grace standing a few feet away.

"We've been together since before seven. Had dinner at Doc's, then went to Thorn's house. He never left."

Rick stared at her a moment, as if debating whether to ask more questions, then shook his head. "All right." He scribbled in a pad, then looked back at Thorn. "Anyone have a beef with you guys? Maybe threaten you?"

"No one." Thorn ran a hand through his hair. "The shop's been open a couple weeks. Not enough time to create any enemies."

"What about from high school? I understand you grew up here."

Josh snickered. "That would be a helluva long time to hold a grudge."

"It's been known to happen." Rick slid the pad and pen into a pocket.

Grace stood next to Thorn, her hand reaching out to clutch his. "Rick, shouldn't we wait for the arson investigator's report?"

"I was told she'd been sent to another fire. They're checking for someone else. If not, she might not be able to get here until sometime late tomorrow."

"Dammit." Tony crossed his arms, watching a group of firefighters rush toward the back of the garage. "That means it'll be a couple days before they'll allow us into the building."

Before anyone could respond, a car pulled up and stopped. Relief rushed through Thorn when Jillian Somerville stepped out and walked toward them.

"Gentlemen. I wish I could say it's good to see you again." She shook everyone's hand, then looked at Grace. "They replaced me on a fire in Missoula so I could come here." Taking a moment to glance at the flames, she shook her head. "Someone's sure trying to get our attention."

"What makes you say that?" Rick asked, lifting a brow.

"I don't believe in coincidences, Detective. Two fires in this short a time have to be related."

"Ms. Somerville, this is Grace Jackson. Grace, this is Jillian Somerville. She's the arson investigator." Grace and Jillian shook hands before Jillian shifted toward the building.

"There may not be much for me to do right now, but I'll check out what I can." Jillian took a few pictures before walking away.

If his shop wasn't being destroyed by the fire, Thorn might have found the look Grace gave Jillian comical. "She's not what we expected, either."

Grace shot a look at him, an eyebrow raised. "Oh really?"

Sighing, he tightened his hold on her hand. "Did Wolf find you?"

"Yeah." She breathed the word out on a heavy sigh. "You told him we're back together."

This wasn't what he wanted to talk about. Not here. Not now. He didn't take his focus off the garage. "Is that a problem?"

She shook her head. "Not for me. I think it might be for him."

Thorn glanced down at her, feeling a jolt of satisfaction at seeing their joined hands. "What did he say?"

"He gave me an ultimatum. Take the promotion in Austin or else."

Thorn narrowed his eyes. "Or else what?"

"I'll be looking for new employment."

Chapter Eleven

No one left until well after sunup, including Grace, who sat on a bench across the street, holding a cup of coffee. Evie had brought enough for everyone, including donuts and bagels. Grace could barely swallow the coffee without feeling sick. It wasn't the brew making her stomach churn. The hollow look on Thorn's face as he, Josh, and Tony surveyed the damage ripped at her heart.

They'd put everything they had into this venture. Grace knew not one of them would give up. It wasn't in their nature to turn and run, yet the task before them must seem daunting after all their hard work over the last few weeks.

By eight o'clock, Jillian began investigating. She'd determined arson had been the cause of the first fire, and without saying as much, gave Thorn the impression she expected to determine the same for the second.

Two hours later, she walked up to him, a grim expression on her face.

"What did you find?"

Jillian looked at him, her eyes narrowing and voice just above a whisper. "This is off the record until the report is filed. Understand?"

Shoving his hands into his pockets, he nodded. "Yeah."

"Same as the last one. Whoever did this used gasoline mixed with either motor oil or diesel. The last fire showed a small amount of accelerant and was set outside the block wall at the back. That's why you had so little damage. This time, a greater quantity of accelerant was used, and the point of origin was on the side where the building is made of wood." She closed her tablet, biting her lower lip as she scanned the area one more time. "My guess is this is an amateur getting back at you for some perceived wrong. He or she doesn't want to hurt anyone, but is making a point. My suggestion is for you to sit down with Reyes and Coletti. Make a list of anyone who might have a grudge against one of you." Jillian looked past Thorn to see Rick Zoeller approaching. "The detective is on his way over. I'm sure he'll tell you the same."

"Any news, Ms. Somerville?" Rick glanced between the two, but couldn't discern anything from the solemn expressions.

"I'll have the full report out by later today, but I can confirm it's arson. I've advised Mr. Macklin that you'd want a list of people who might have it out for him or one of his partners."

Rick nodded, not surprised. "Yeah, I suspected as much." He looked at Thorn. "I'd like the list as soon as possible. You might want to consider hiring a security guard to watch the place at night and on weekends when one of you isn't here. It's up to you."

"I've got a call in to my brother." Thorn had tried to reach Del twice, but knew his brother was out of town at some statewide sheriff convention.

"If the sheriff doesn't know of someone, I can ask the police chief. Ex-military are good, too."

Thorn agreed, already having an idea of who to contact. "Thanks, Detective. I'll get you the list by tonight, but don't expect much. Tony, Josh, and I all had our share of run-ins with kids in high school, but nothing major that I can recall. Since then?" He shrugged. Not one name came to mind, and he doubted there'd be much from Josh or Tony.

"What about family? Each of you should consider who might have a grudge against a family member. Arsonists think in strange ways and their targets don't always make sense."

"He's right, Thorn." Jillian slipped on her sunglasses, watching Josh and Tony walk toward them. "There are all kinds of motivations for someone to start a fire, and it may not be that they're after you specifically. Some arsonists believe they can get back at someone by hurting a person they love."

"So if someone were after Del for putting them in jail, they might come after me, or even my other brother, Boone?" Thorn shut his eyes, thinking of the possibilities. "I'll talk to Boone and Del, and ask Josh and Tony to speak to their families. Still, it's doubtful the list will be more than a few names."

Rick smirked. "I only need one—as long as it's the right one."

A soft knock had Grace looking up from her desk. Thorn stood in the doorway, a sack from Evie's in his hand. Holding it up, he walked toward her.

"I brought lunch."

Coming around the desk, she placed a soft kiss on his lips. "I'm not sure how hungry I am, but it's worth a try. Sit down." She nodded at the two guest chairs. "Do you want some water or a soda?"

"Water would be good."

"I'll be right back."

When she walked out, Thorn took the time to glance around her office, seeing nothing indicating she had a family, friends, or a life outside Gray Wolf Outfitters. It was in sharp contrast to what he remembered of Grace when they were teenagers. In those days, her bedroom walls didn't have an inch of free space. Posters, pictures, movie and concert tickets were plastered everywhere, including her closet door. Shelves were cluttered with framed images of her family, her girlfriends, Thorn, and an oversized framed image of Grace, Thorn, and Mr. Weiker. She even had a couple of Thorn's trophies on her desk.

This office held no trace of the Grace he'd known all those years ago. Cold and impersonal, the image she wanted to show the world. Or was it the image Wolf expected of her?

"Here you are." She handed him a bottle of water, unaware of the thoughts running through his mind. Grabbing the bag he'd set on her desk, she peeked inside, raising a brow. "Wraps?"

Pulling the sack from her hand, Thorn took out one of the wraps. "Can't a guy eat something healthy?"

Her mouth twitched as she snatched the bag from his grip. "Sure. I just didn't expect you to be one of those guys." Removing hers, something at the bottom caught her attention. Pulling it out, she held it in the air. "A chocolate and nut bar?"

A smile tugged at his lips. "Nuts are healthy. You'd be surprised how many of my team members carried those things."

"Right. Like you've never had a sweet tooth." She bit into the wrap as her stomach growled.

"Guess you needed food more than you thought." He took a large bite, groaning in pleasure. "Evie sure does know how to cook."

They ate in silence until Thorn finished, wadding the wrapper into a ball. He'd come to ask a favor, as well as bring lunch. Now he hesitated. It had been years since they'd been together, Grace witnessing a few of the unusual instances when he'd gotten in someone's face or vice versa. He doubted she'd have anything to add to the meager list he, Josh, and Tony had prepared.

"So, what do you need?"

His eyes widened in feigned innocence.

Smiling, she shook her head. "Don't try to fool me, Thorn. You're sweet to bring lunch, but I don't think you'd risk coming into Wolf's den without a very good reason."

Laughing, he reached over, grabbing her hand. "It's been years since I've heard that expression."

"You're lucky. I use it all the time." Her smile faded. "Tell me how I can help."

He studied her face, knowing there was more to the way she'd closed up. Leaning forward, he tucked a strand of hair behind her ear. "Your detective wants a list of anyone who might be angry enough to set two fires."

Her face tightened. "He's not *my* detective."

Scrubbing a hand down his face, he let out a breath. "I know. I'm being hard on the guy because I know you're dating him."

Grace's lips parted. She squeezed his hand. "We only went out a few times."

"And?"

Cocking her head, her brows furrowed. "Are you asking me if I slept with him?"

Squirming in his chair, he shook his head. "It's none of my business."

"No, it's not." Pursing her lips, she leveled a hard stare at him. "And no, I didn't. We decided not to see each other again for a lot of reasons, none of which I'm going to share with you." Standing, she walked behind her desk and sat down. "Do you already have a list started?"

Nodding, he pulled it from his pocket, handing it to her. "There isn't much. He asked us to include anyone who might have problems with any members of our families."

Reading the short list, she looked up. "Makes sense. Get at them through one of you." Picking up her pen, she tapped it on her desk a few times, shaking her head. "You've put down the ones I would think of. Well, except for one." She glanced at him, her eyes filled with alarm.

"Don't even think it, Grace."

"I have to. You and I both know what he's capable of." Rubbing her temples with her fingers, she let out a groan.

Moving around the desk, he crouched next to her, settling an arm across her shoulders. "Babe, listen to me. Keeping his teenage daughter away from a boy he didn't think would amount to much is a helluva lot different than arson."

Her stomach knotted at how angry Wolf was when he'd learned they were back together. "He threatened to fire me if I didn't take the job in Austin."

Sucking in a breath, Thorn blew it out as he planned his next words. "I love you, Grace. That will never change. But maybe he's right. He's offering a great opportunity in a dynamic city, running your own shop with a salary I can only hope to earn one day."

The knot in her stomach moved to her throat, tightening until she found it hard to breathe. Forcing herself, she whispered what she feared. "So you want me to take it."

135

"I want you to be happy, Grace. If accepting the promotion is what's best for you, then yes, you should take it."

Shaking off his arm, she stood, looking down at him. "I don't have any other names to add to your list." Walking to the door, she pulled it open. "I've a full schedule the rest of the day, so I'd better get back to it." She'd been a fool to believe he loved her enough to ask her to stay, and if she didn't back away now, her heart would be crushed one more time.

Standing, he met her at the door. "All right." Clearing his throat, he glanced around once more, still confused by the lack of anything personal, unaware of the pain radiating through her. "You don't have any pictures of your family or friends."

"I've chosen not to bring them here. Thanks again for lunch."

Thorn leaned down, meaning to kiss her, until she drew away. Tilting his head, he watched her pull into herself. "Will I see you tonight?"

Hugging her arms around her waist, she shook her head. "I need to make a decision about Austin. It's better if I do that alone."

"Whatever's best for you, Grace."

Watching him turn and walk down the hall caused a crushing pain so acute she bent over before closing the door. Leaning her back against it, Grace swiped at the tears pooling in her eyes. She knew he loved her—just not enough to ask her to turn down the offer and stay in Whiskey Bend.

Maybe her father was right and Thorn wasn't the right man for her. If he were, he'd do everything possible to make her stay, never letting her go. Instead, he'd given up.

Closing her eyes, she tilted her head back against the door, as miserable now as she had been all those years ago. Grace didn't know what she'd decide, except she had no intention of going through the same pain again.

Thorn had returned to town because of promises he'd made to himself and an important teacher a long time ago. With or without her, he would make his dream happen. She now had a decision to make. Take the promotion and lose another part of herself, or find the courage to pursue her own dream, even if it meant going after it alone.

Dropping the wrench, Thorn mumbled an oath as he cradled his injured hand. For five days, they'd been cleaning up after the fire, making repairs, and waiting to hear if Detective Zoeller had come up with any suspects. He'd also been waiting the same length of time to hear from Grace.

Phone messages, several texts, and numerous emails had gone unanswered. Her lack of response had gotten to him within hours of leaving the first message. By now, he was beyond frustrated. Thorn had tried to do the right thing, encouraging her to follow her dream and take the promotion. Maybe he should've kept his mouth shut.

"Another owie, boss?" Josh stood over him, holding back a chuckle. "That's what? The fourth since we got back into the garage?"

"Bug off, Josh." He wanted to respond differently, not daring with Tony a few feet away talking to potential clients—a husband and wife referred to Scorpion by Ian Hardesty. "I've got a lot on my mind."

"Yeah. We all do. Doesn't mean we have to tear ourselves up. I'll get the first aid kit."

"Get back to what you were doing. I can take care of this myself." Pulling out a handkerchief, he wrapped it around his hand, grumbling about his own stupidity as he stalked off.

"I'll give you a little time to talk about how you'd like to proceed. Excuse me." Tony smiled at the middle-aged couple who wanted similar bikes for a cross-country road trip planned in six months. Stopping next to the bike Thorn had been working on—the one Thorn planned on giving to Grace, he shook his head at the few drops of blood on the floor. He glanced at Josh. "Another accident?"

"Number four by my count. Something's up with Thorn, and I don't think it has to do with the latest fire."

They'd been surprised how well the conversation with the insurance company had gone. It helped their agent had been a friend in high school and a motorcycle enthusiast. She'd already gone over plans to update her current ride with some changes and a new paint job.

Tony crossed his arms, glancing over his shoulder at the couple, who spoke in whispers. "I thought the fact Hardesty didn't blink at the second fire, and sent us a customer, would've improved his mood. Guess there's only one person who can do that."

"And I don't think she's talking." Josh tossed a rag aside.

They'd worked non-stop to get the showroom and office cleaned, repainted, and operational within three days, allowing the last two days to work on repairing bikes. During the chaos, the fire appeared worse than it was. Most damage occurred in the back garage, where a couple motorcycles awaited repairs. Those would be covered by insurance. If all went well, their owners would have them in their possession within another week.

Miraculously, the bikes in the showroom suffered minor damage, most able to be repaired with detailed cleaning and new paint. Before leaving for the gun range on Sunday, Thorn had rolled Grace's bike alongside those in the front. The move had spared it. He still had a great deal of work to do before handing it off to Josh.

Tony opened his mouth to say something when he saw Thorn walking back up. Looking down, he couldn't miss the bruising or swelling. "Do you need stitches? I can take you to the hospital."

Sighing, Thorn shook his head. "Nah. It looks worse than it is. I'm going over to Evie's. Can I bring back anything for you guys?"

Josh jumped at the chance for food. "A burger with everything. No. Make it two."

Tony chuckled. For a tall, wiry man, Josh sure could pack food away. "I'll go over after I'm finished with our new customers. Onion breath doesn't work when I'm trying to close a deal."

"Noted."

Grabbing the cowboy hat he'd owned before joining the army, Thorn stepped outside, looking up at the bright midday sun. Feeling like a stalker, he'd been to Evie's every day, hoping to see Grace. He'd walked by the Gray Wolf offices several times, spotting her car in the lot, and even drove by her house. He'd yet to get a glimpse of her.

At the time, he thought she needed a couple days to sort out her future. Thorn now believed he'd made a mess of things with his attempt to be supportive. If she'd return his calls or answer his texts, he'd get her to meet him, maybe figure this out together. Instead, she'd chosen to cut him off.

Chapter Twelve

Stepping through the entrance of the diner, Thorn stopped when his gaze landed on Grace. She sat in one of the booths, Wolf sitting across from her. Her features were hard, eyes cold, lips pressed into a thin line. He stared at her, knowing she hadn't noticed him, wondering what had her so upset. Thorn didn't have to wait long.

Taking a few steps forward, he halted when Wolf stood, both hands on the table as he leaned toward Grace and said something. When finished, he turned, his gaze boring into Thorn's as he pushed past him and walked outside.

After watching Wolf's retreat, Thorn turned back to Grace, who stared at him, her face awash in misery. Shaking her head, she glanced over at Evie, who seemed to nod in understanding, then looked back to see Thorn slipping into the booth across from her.

"Are you all right?"

"No. Yes." Taking a breath, she exhaled. "I don't know."

Thorn leaned forward, resting his arms on the table. "Do you want to talk about it?"

"Not now, and definitely not here." When she stood, he started to rise. "Stay and have lunch. I need some alone time." As she walked past, he grabbed her wrist, stopping her.

"It's been five days without a response from you, Grace."

"I know," she hissed, aware of other diners staring at them, still upset at how the conversation with her father had ended. "Now isn't the time. I'll come to the shop after I leave my office. Will you have time to talk to me then?"

"I'll make time."

"Blackstar is the best at providing security services, Thorn. If I call, they'll have someone out tonight." Del walked through the back garage, noting the damage inside and also the point of origin identified on the arson report. Although the police had jurisdiction, as the sheriff, he often worked with the chief and his people. Del didn't expect any pushback since the arson involved his family.

"Thanks. We've taken turns watching the shop the last week. I've got to say, I could use some professional help. And some sleep."

Waiting until Del completed the call, arranging for a guard to arrive before they closed, Thorn turned back toward the showroom, taking a mental note of what still needed to get done for the shop to be back to normal. Following Del into the front, he watched his brother walk from bike to bike, stopping at the Sportster.

Studying it, a grin tugged at the corners of his brother's mouth. "She's going to be a beauty when you're finished. Is this the one you're working on for Grace?"

Thorn stilled. He hadn't mentioned being back with her to either of his brothers. When he didn't respond, Del glanced up.

"Josh mentioned you'd picked up an old Harley. I guessed about it being for Grace. Of course, that was after Wolf cornered me at the grocery, intimating you were back together."

Thorn's jaw hardened. "What else did he say?"

"Not much, except he hoped Grace didn't throw away a golden opportunity for an old boyfriend—or something like that. What did he mean?" Del crossed his arms, leaning against the front window frame.

"Who the hell knows. The man has a way of saying things that make sense at first, then get turned around when you study them more."

"I hear you. What opportunity does Grace have?" Del didn't move from his spot.

"Wolf offered her a promotion to vice president at a new facility in Austin. More money, house, autonomy—"

Del laughed at that.

"I know, but at least she'd be several states away without him dropping into her office several times each day." He blew out a breath, still berating himself for pushing Grace to take the job. "I told her it was a good opportunity. She's pushed me away ever since."

"So I take it you two *did* get back together."

"Where'd you hear that?"

Del shook his head, grinning. "Have you already forgotten how small Whiskey Bend is and how much the people love new gossip? Especially when it involves a war hero and the daughter of one of the town's most prominent citizens."

Groaning, Thorn shoved a hand through his hair. "I'm no hero and you know it. Just a guy trying to make a living in his hometown."

"And reconnect with the girl he left behind. I've never figured out why Wolf had it out for you, and maybe he still does. Back in the day, you two were pretty tight. Closer than you were to our own father."

"It's no mystery. He finally figured out I wasn't good enough for Grace. Hell, I could've told him that, but he never had the courage to confront me about it. Instead, he lied to me. And to Grace."

"With the help of dear ol' Dad," Del muttered. It was old news to Boone and him, but not to Thorn.

Thorn's eyes flashed. "What do you mean?"

"You never knew about the deal between Wolf and Pop. No one did until a few months before he and Mom died." Del glanced behind Thorn, looking into the office. "Do you have any whiskey stashed in there?"

Looking over his shoulder as he headed toward the desk, Thorn nodded. "Always."

Pulling the almost full bottle from a drawer, he grabbed two cups, pouring until they each held about three fingers. Handing one to Del, he leaned against the desk, waiting for news he didn't want to hear.

Taking a sip, Del raised his eyebrows. "Good stuff."

"Even an army grunt can afford this once in a while. Now, tell me what it is I don't know."

"I doubt any of it will surprise you. Neither Pop nor Wolf wanted you and Grace together. They didn't interfere while you were in high school, figuring the relationship would burn itself out. When it didn't, they formed a plan. Wolf would tell you Grace left town, and tell her you'd taken off. Deciding you weren't ready to be tied down, Pop was to match Wolf's story, believing it would force you to accept his ultimatum about working the ranch or going to college. Pop about had a heart attack when you enlisted."

Thorn palmed the cup, staring at the amber liquid. "Grace told me about Wolf. She didn't mention Pop."

Del shrugged. "With him gone, she might have decided it was better to leave that part in the past."

Closing his eyes, Thorn absorbed what Del had said. "Wolf hated me that much?"

"I doubt he ever hated you. Like any father, he wanted to protect his daughter from what he saw as a bleak future. And Pop agreed. The fact is, Pop made Wolf an offer he couldn't refuse."

Thorn licked his lips, not sure how much more he wanted to hear. "What offer?"

"The property where Gray Wolf Outfitters has its headquarters belonged to Pop. For Wolf's promise to get Grace out of town, he practically gave it to him."

Before Thorn could comment, Del held up his hand. "There's more. After they died, Boone and I went through Pop's and Mom's things, including paperwork at least thirty years old. I don't know how much Mom knew, but Pop kept a record of everything, including what appeared to be some real shady business dealings." Del pinched the bridge of his nose. "Hell, we always knew Pop wasn't a saint. The truth is, Thorn, he may have been involved in some criminal activities."

Thorn let out a breath. He'd suspected as much a few times after hearing comments in town, but never confronted his father. "Anything specific?"

"Extortion, fraud, a little theft here and there. You know, your average low-life stuff." Del's attempt at humor fell flat as the bitterness in his voice grew stronger with each word. "The fool documented almost all of it. I wasn't the sheriff yet when Boone and I discovered the truth. Knowing what happened, I almost didn't run for office."

"That would've been a mistake. You're the best sheriff this county has ever had. Besides, what Pop did had no bearing on you."

Del shook his head. "I never reported any of it. Boone and I couldn't even track down any of the victims."

Thorn's brows knitted together. "You said he wrote it all down."

"Not names or places. Just activities and amounts. The best we could tell, the last one was at least ten years before you graduated from high school, and fifteen years for the one before that. We found the documents over twenty years after the last entry. Talk about a cold trail with no leads."

Thorn stiffened. "Do you think he pulled any of this crap on people in Whiskey Bend?"

"It's doubtful. Believe me, the sheriff's election was rough. If any locals got caught up in his dealings, it would've spread all over. I held my breath until the vote tally, but nothing surfaced. Still, I felt lousy about what our old man did."

"I was about fifteen, you were thirteen, and Boone was eleven when he posted the last entry."

"As best as we can tell, yes. And before you say it, I already understand we weren't responsible and have no way of making things right." He thumped his own head, then held a fisted hand to his chest. "But in here, his actions still haunt me."

Thorn shook his head, snorting. "Keeping Grace and I apart was a walk in the park for the man."

"Pretty much." Del drained the cup, setting it on the desk. "He could be a real S.O.B., but I never expected to find what he'd hidden in the attic."

"What did you do with it?"

"We hauled it all to the old storage shed near the barn."

Thorn's eyes widened. "The one that burned down in the lightning storm?"

"One and the same." Standing, Del looked at his older brother. "What's done is done, including what he did to push you and Grace apart. If she's who you want, don't let anyone stand in your way this time."

Grace checked her watch, frustration building at the additional paperwork shuffled her way. She knew why, also knowing who had approved the extra burden be given to her instead of an assistant.

Wolf had become determined to do all he could to force her to make the move he wanted. She'd been wavering, seriously considering the promotion, until his actions made it clear he wanted her out of Whiskey Bend and far away from Thorn.

Shuffling through the stacks of paper, her eyes glazing as the words ran together, it became crystal clear what she wanted. A new energy surged through her, an uplifting feeling she hadn't felt in a long time.

Not allowing herself any time to reconsider, Grace shoved the papers aside. Grabbing two empty file boxes from the closet in her office, she picked up one stack after another. Within minutes, her desk was clean. The weight coloring her judgment for years disappeared the instant she secured the lid on the last box.

She didn't need to go to Austin to follow her dream, nor did she need Wolf to support or understand her decision. Most of all, she didn't need Thorn pushing her toward a dream that wasn't hers. She shared the blame. Still, he'd never asked what she wanted or if she enjoyed her work. Like Wolf, he assumed she'd found her calling. Because you were good at something didn't mean it should be your life's work.

Would Thorn support the change? Either he would or he wouldn't.

Without acknowledging it, she'd been moving in this direction for weeks. Researching degrees and credentials at the University of Montana, she'd been overjoyed to find out her dream could be achieved less than two hours away. She hoped to commute two or three days a week, filling the rest of her schedule with online classes.

She refused to approach her father for part-time work. Evie had already offered her a waitress job and would work around her school schedule. It wouldn't amount to much. Coupled with her savings, she'd make out all right. If all else failed, she'd rent out her house, find another place to live and employment in Missoula until she achieved her goal.

Setting the boxes along one wall, grimacing at the late time, she grabbed her purse. Tomorrow, she'd hand in her notice, clean out her desk, and have a sense of self for the first time since her father sent Thorn away and vanquished her to a life back east.

Thorn glanced at his watch. Seven o'clock and Grace still hadn't shown up. Blackstar's security man arrived at six, checked the interior, walked the perimeter, made a few suggestions, then began patrolling outside. Ex-army and all business, he and Thorn had hit it off right away.

His stomach growled. Setting aside the tools he'd been using on the Harley, he grabbed a tarp, covering the bike. If Grace did show up, he didn't want her to see it. When the hunger pains flashed again, he made the decision to leave. She'd either forgotten their discussion or didn't find the need to talk with him all that important. Either way, it didn't bode well for their future.

Grabbing his keys, Thorn took one more look around, leaving on the security lights and those highlighting the bikes in the showroom. He'd say a couple words to the guard, then mount his bike. Cooking for himself didn't appeal, and Evie's had become a habit. Thorn figured the Mexican restaurant a few blocks from the edge of town had a carne asada burrito with his name on it.

Closing and locking the door, he glanced down the street toward the Gray Wolf building. A few offices still had their lights on. Grace's wasn't one of them. He'd almost made it around the corner of the building when he heard someone shouting his name. Turning, he saw Grace dashing toward him, slowing to a fast walk as she got closer.

"I had a few things to finish. They took longer than I thought." Stopping in front of him, she dragged in a breath, her eyes sparkling as her lips curved into a slight smile. "Sorry. I should've called you."

He almost laughed, wondering what had her so excited. "You don't look sorry."

"It's just..." She caught her lower lip between her teeth, glancing down at her feet.

Reaching out, he lifted her chin until her gaze locked with his. His gut clenched when he saw the shimmer of tears in her eyes. "It's just what, Grace?"

Swiping the moisture from her face, she blinked a few times. "Do you have your bike?"

His eyes crinkled at the corners. "I do."

"Can we ride?"

"Whatever you want, Grace." Grabbing her hand, he had her next to his bike in seconds.

Strapping on the helmet and slipping into the jacket he handed her, she climbed behind him, wrapping her arms around his waist as he started the engine. An instant later, they were on the road, heading to wherever Thorn wanted to take them.

Chapter Thirteen

Thorn knew where he wanted to go. He remembered the last time they'd taken this ride using an old bike he worked on every day. They were seventeen with their entire lives ahead of them, having no worries and no clue how everything would change within a few weeks.

Settling his left hand over Grace's clasped around his waist, he squeezed, more than grateful she'd come to him tonight. Something big had happened, and he wanted to hear every detail. For now, he'd wait, give her time to relax, enjoy the night air, and form her thoughts.

Thorn could hear her startled gasp when he turned into the take-out burger place she loved. She didn't wait to climb off and dash inside, all smiles as he walked up beside her.

Grace knew exactly what she wanted. "Double cheeseburger with everything and seasoned fries. Oh, and a chocolate malt with extra malt."

He looked her up and down, admiring her slim figure and so much more. "You think you can handle a load like that, sweetheart?"

"Positive." She almost buzzed with excitement as he placed the same order for both of them, replacing her malt with a soda for him. "Where are we going?"

Crossing his arms, he placed his feet shoulder width apart. "It's a surprise."

Her gaze narrowed as her mind ticked through the possibilities. He knew she'd figured it out when her eyes widened. "Falls Cave." She sang out the words, her eyes sparkling with excitement.

Shaking his head, he didn't acknowledge her guess one way or the other. "Guess you'll have to wait and see."

She walked up to him. "We're taking dinner with us, right?"

"Yes." He cocked his head.

She bounced on the balls of her feet. "Then it's Falls Cave."

The corners of his mouth curved into a grin.

"You aren't going to tell me, are you?" She placed her hands on his chest, gripping the flannel shirt.

Looking down, he liked seeing her hands on him, liked seeing the excitement on her face. "Nope."

A worker placed a bag on the counter. "Order for Macklin."

She snatched the sack and dashed outside, securing her helmet before he even reached the bike.

"Seems I've got a hungry woman on my hands." Climbing on the bike, he waited until Grace got on behind him, settling the bag between her legs. "Ready?"

She tapped his shoulder in response, then clasped her hands around his waist.

Thirty minutes later, they took the short path from the gravel cutout off the highway, making their way to the falls. The sound of running water got louder as they closed in on their destination—the hidden caves behind the falls.

Hidden was relative since generations of kids knew of its existence, using it as a place to get away from the prying eyes of adults. Some towns had a lookout, others a point, still others a secluded spot in the woods. The kids of Whiskey Bend had Falls Cave.

"I can't believe you brought me here."

He stopped on the trail, waiting for her to turn around. It took a good minute before she realized he wasn't behind her.

She walked back toward him, her face somber. "Is something wrong?"

Taking the bag from her hand, he set it on the ground, then snaked an arm around her. Leaning down, he crushed his mouth to hers, kissing her until they had to break away, breathless.

Grace touched a finger to her lips. "Wow," she breathed out.

"Yeah...wow. It's been almost a week, which is about six days too long." He pulled her back against him, claiming her mouth again, going a little slower this time, savoring the feel of her in his arms. "Grace," he whispered against her lips as his hands moved down her back to settle on her waist. It would be so easy to find a clearing and spread out their jackets, but the gurgling sound coming from Grace's stomach had them both chuckling.

"Sorry..." She placed a hand on her stomach. "I didn't eat much at lunch."

Picking up the bag, Thorn threaded his fingers through hers, placing a kiss on the tip of her nose. "Let's find the cave and get some food in you."

The sound of the falls grew louder as they wound their way up the hill. Stopping at a lookout, Thorn pulled her in front of him and wrapped his arms around her waist, drawing her against his chest, resting his chin on the top of her head.

"This is one of my favorite views."

Thorn's lips tilted up into a grin. "That's why I stopped." Leaning down, he kissed the sensitive spot below her ear, then trailed kisses down her neck to her shoulder.

"Mmm, that feels good. Why don't we eat here?"

"Are we talking about food?" he mumbled against her neck as he made his way back up to her ear. "Because if we're not..."

Laughing, she turned in his arms, placing her hands on his chest. "Food. I really do need food."

"Then we need to get to the cave. Once we settle in to eat, I don't plan on leaving for a while."

Grace raised a brow. "Using food to get to my body, are you?"

His face sobered. "Truthfully, I'm using food to get you to talk to me."

She let out a breath, placing her hand in his. "You're right. I owe you an explanation about what's going on. Let me eat my burger, then I promise we'll talk."

"About everything, Grace. It's time to get everything out."

Shoving down the lump in her throat, she nodded.

Letting out a satisfied sigh, Grace crumbled the wrapper into a ball, tossing it at Thorn before she laid back on the jackets they'd spread on the ground. "That was heavenly."

Stretching out beside her, he leaned over, swiping strands of hair from her face. "You didn't finish your fries."

Closing her eyes, she let herself relax. "Who says I'm finished?"

He studied her, knowing Grace would be asleep in moments if he didn't intervene. "Hey. There's no chance I'm letting you nod off until we've talked."

Leaving her eyes closed, her lips curved up at the corners. "I can talk lying down."

"Not from my experience. Come on, sweetheart. It's time to sit up." Ignoring her groan, Thorn stood up, then sat down behind her, drawing her up to rest between his legs, leaning her back against his chest. "You comfortable?"

"Hmm?"

Shaking his head, he chuckled before kissing the top of her head. "I've given you plenty of time, Grace. You need to tell me what had you so excited this evening." He could feel her tense slightly, then relax again as she let out a deep breath.

"I made a decision."

Thorn's chest tightened. He didn't want to lose her to a job in Austin. At the same time, he wanted her to be free to reach her goals, the same as he was trying to do. Nothing ever came easy.

"And?"

"When I go in tomorrow, I'm turning in my resignation."

He didn't respond at first, sucking in a slow breath to steady his reaction.

"Nothing to say to that?"

He could hear the disappointment in her voice, the implied censure. "I'm just surprised. I thought you wanted the promotion."

Her body tensed an instant before she stood up, turning to look down at him as she crossed her arms.

"Wolf wanted me to take it, and you encouraged me to go along with it. The thing is, no one ever asked *me* if it was what I wanted."

Glancing away from the obvious accusation, he thought of the few times she'd mentioned the promotion, chastising himself. She was right.

"I assumed after all your hard work…" Shaking his head, he pushed himself up. "I'm sorry, Grace." His stomach tightened when he saw the disillusion in her eyes.

Turning her back to him, she walked toward the falls. The cave behind the falling water went deep into the mountain. They'd explored it more than once, going no more than a couple hundred feet before turning back. She loved it here, and as senseless as it was, always thought of it as their spot. Sensing Thorn walk up behind her, she wrapped her arms around her waist.

"When we were in high school, do you remember our plans?" She grimaced at the melancholy sound of her voice.

"Yes."

"You wanted to own your own custom motorcycle shop. Be the best in Montana and the entire northwestern region." She turned to face him, her eyes glistening with moisture, even as a wistful smile crossed her face.

"Yes. Things changed, Grace."

"No. My father forced us to change our plans."

"Don't you mean *our* fathers?" He smirked, seeing her eyes go wide. "Del told me what my father did, the deal he made with Wolf for the land in town if he went along with the plan to separate us."

"I hate that building." Stepping a few paces away, she turned to face the waterfall once more. "It's been tough to walk inside each day, knowing how he'd gotten the land to build Gray Wolf headquarters."

"He told you that part?"

"No. Mother let it slip one afternoon when we were working in her garden. She spoke as if it wasn't an issue, hadn't changed the course of my life and yours." Grace sucked in a shaky breath. "She told me it was for the best. Not only did our fathers end a foolish, youthful infatuation, the Jackson family got a ridiculously cheap deal on prime land. She knew about it all along, Thorn. Her confession made me sick."

Anger pulsed through him, understanding the sense of betrayal she felt at her parents' actions. He felt the same bitterness toward his father, as well as disgust at the pattern of deceit and illegal activities that defined the man's life.

Placing his hands on her shoulders, he felt her resist when he tried to draw her back to him. "I'm sorry they deceived you...deceived us, Grace. They took years away from us. Time we'll never get back." Ignoring her rigid stance, he pulled her to him, wrapping his arms around her waist. "It doesn't mean we can't be together now. If you are going to quit, we'll have plenty of time to work things out between us. I love you—"

"I'm going back to school in Missoula. I want to be a teacher."

When she tried to break his hold this time, he let her, his arms dropping to his sides as she spun to face him. The look on his face had hers drawing into a frown.

"What are you looking so smug about?"

Her question took him by surprise. "Did you think I wouldn't be happy about your decision?" Dragging a hand through his hair, he paced a few feet away, then turned back to face her. "Hell, Grace, you always wanted to teach. Missoula isn't that far away. A whole lot closer than Austin."

Lines of confusion appeared around her eyes. "You don't care if I stay in Whiskey Bend?"

"What are you talking about? If I had my way, we'd already be picking a wedding date."

Her lips parted. "A wedding date?"

Stepping closer, Thorn took her hands in his. "Tomorrow works for me. Or next week, if that's better for you."

"I thought..."

He cocked his head. "Thought what?"

She shook her head. "You seemed so set on me taking the promotion and moving away. I thought you'd changed your mind about us."

"Never. I've always known you were who I wanted. Since I first saw you in grade school, you were it for me." Tugging her to him, he wrapped his arms around her. "I love you. Marry me, Grace."

Her heart squeezed. She'd dreamed of hearing these words so many times, convincing herself it would never happen. "Are you sure?"

She felt a rumble in his chest. "I've never been more sure of anything."

"What about school?"

"What about it? Whatever it takes, whatever I can do to help you, we'll make it work. I'm not letting you go again. Not ever." He chuckled as a thought occurred to him.

She glanced up, seeing the gleam in his eyes. "What's so funny?"

"Just thinking about how, one day, you might even be the teacher for our children."

"Our children," she whispered.

"Of course, it all hinges on if you agree to marry me."

A slow smile spread across her face, a lone tear slipping down her cheek. "You're it for me, too, Thorn. Yes, I'll marry you."

Chapter Fourteen

Grace remained standing, hands clasped in front of her, as Wolf read her resignation letter. She knew the instant it all clicked into place for him. A deep growl began low in his throat before he looked up, his eyes on fire.

"What is this." It wasn't a question as much as a demand.

Her features didn't change as her gaze met his and held. "I've decided to leave Gray Wolf. That is my letter of resignation."

"I know what it is, Grace. I want to know why." He motioned toward a chair in front of his desk. "And would you please sit down."

She'd known this wouldn't be easy. At least he hadn't yelled at her...yet. Sighing, she settled into a chair, her back rigid.

Setting down the letter, Wolf leaned forward, resting his arms on the desk. "Why leave?"

"I don't know why this is such a surprise to you, Father."

Shaking his head, he let out an exasperated sigh. "Is this about Thorn?"

"This is about what I want, which has nothing to do with Thorn." She had no plans to tell him they'd agreed to marry, and were already considering dates. Whether in a church or a civil ceremony, her parents would be invited to the wedding, although she doubted they'd attend.

162

"It's always been about that boy."

"He's a grown man, with the medals to prove it, and whether or not you like it, I love him. At one time, so did you. No matter what you've said in the past, I don't understand why you hate him."

Slapping his palms on the desk, Wolf stood, bending toward her. "I don't hate Thorn." Blowing out a breath, he walked around the desk, resting his hip against it.

Grace didn't believe him. "You have a strange way of showing it." Her father didn't like Thorn, had turned on him fourteen years ago and done nothing to welcome him back to Whiskey Bend now. "Regardless, my decision to quit has nothing to do with him."

"Have you gotten an offer somewhere else? If it's about money, we can negotiate."

Biting her lip so she wouldn't say something she'd regret, Grace stood and paced to the window. Crossing her arms, she worked to calm the irritation flowing through her. Wolf always believed work was about money or a fancy title. He never understood the part about liking your job. She couldn't remember a time when he'd ever asked her what she wanted.

"It isn't about money, Father."

"Then what, Grace?"

Licking her lips, she hesitated, already knowing how he'd react. Steeling herself, she turned back toward him. "I'm going back to school. I want to be a teacher."

Pinching the bridge of his nose, he looked at her. "For the love of...I thought you put those thoughts behind you years ago."

"I never put them behind me. I'll admit they were buried deep, almost too deep to retrieve."

"What made you think of them now?"

"Your offer."

His eyes narrowed, his brows drawing together in confusion. "I thought you'd jump at the chance for your own facility, a job as vice president."

"You assumed I'd jump at the offer. The thing is, you never asked me what I wanted." The fight went out of her, excitement taking its place as she thought of standing up in front of a group of young children. "I want to teach. I've always wanted to teach. Don't you think it's time I went after my own dreams?"

Scrubbing both hands down his face, he stood, walking around the desk again. Lowering himself slowly into the chair, he rested his elbows on the desk, steepling his fingers.

"And this sudden change has nothing to do with Thorn?"

Shaking her head, disturbed by his fixation about her and Thorn, she walked toward the door.

"It has to do with me and no one else. Someday, I hope you'll understand and be happy for me."

Stepping into the hall, she closed the door on a soft click, surprised and thankful he didn't press further.

Entering her office, Grace glanced at her clean desk and the one box of items she'd brought from home. Overall, the meeting had gone better than she'd imagined. The resignation was effective immediately, yet he hadn't said a word to her about it. She refused to feel guilty. At least one employee could take over her job today and move into her office without a misstep in effectiveness. Cross-training had always been a priority at Gray Wolf. Once the seed of change took root, Grace had been diligent in passing her knowledge on to someone else, an employee she knew her father trusted.

Slinging her purse over her shoulder, she picked up the box, taking one more look around. She felt not a twinge of regret.

Excitement engulfed her as she stepped into the elevator, punching the lobby button with a little more enthusiasm than normal. Entering the lobby, a wide grin spread across her face as she shoved through the double glass doors to see a beautiful, cloudless blue sky.

She took a quick glance down the street toward Scorpion, believing Thorn would be inside. Turning toward the parking lot, she stopped. Leaning against her car, his arms crossed, was Thorn.

She took a moment to admire the view. His black t-shirt stretched tight over his chest, his favorite jeans rode low on his hips, and comfortable black leather work boots covered his feet. And he was all hers.

"Hey." He held out his arms, taking the box from her hands.

"Hey, yourself. I thought you'd be at the shop." Unlocking the car, she opened the back door.

"Not when my best girl is starting a new life—with me." Winking at her, he set the box on the back seat. "I thought we could look at rings, then have lunch."

Her throat tightened as warmth spread through her. "In a hurry to get it settled, make sure you caught me?"

Laughing, he took her hand in his, placing a kiss on her knuckles. "Sweetheart, I caught you years ago. It just took a long time to reel you in."

Grace couldn't stop the goofy smile at his silly comment. They used to joke like this all the time, tease each other, laugh until their sides hurt. She still couldn't quite grasp the fact they truly did have a future together.

When he held out his hand, she dropped her keys into his palm. "Let's move your car behind the shop. I want you off Gray Wolf land and onto mine."

She slid inside when Thorn opened the passenger door. Taking one more look at the building, her gaze drifted upward to see Wolf standing at his window, a bland expression on his face as he gazed down at them.

Grace covered her face with both hands, groaning. "I can't decide. They're all gorgeous."

The salesman smiled. "Take your time. This is a big decision—for both of you." Pulling out one more tray of rings, he set it beside the four already on the counter. "Why don't I give you two time to look them over?"

Thorn nodded at the young man. "Thanks."

"I never realized how many decisions go into selecting a wedding set. Gold, platinum, cut of diamond, addition of gemstones. Geez, I don't know why I thought this would be easy."

"Like he said, Grace, take your time. You don't have to decide this minute, as long as we walk out with what we want."

Smiling, she shook her head. "No pressure."

"Absolutely none."

Settling down to business, they picked up a few rings, slipping them on and off, making comments until they had it narrowed down to three engagement rings and four wedding bands.

Thorn tucked a strand of hair behind her ear, kissing her cheek. "We can go someplace else if you aren't sure."

"Not a chance. We're doing this right now." Pursing her lips, she hesitated only an instant before picking up the engagement ring she'd been eyeing the whole time. A gold band with a beautiful marquise diamond accented with blue sapphire stones.

Taking it from her, Thorn slipped it on the ring finger of her left hand, his breath hitching at the sight. "It's beautiful, Grace."

She stared down at it. "We're really doing this, aren't we?"

"Yes, sweetheart. We really are." Leaning down, he kissed her, wanting to do more.

"Did you find one you like?"

They drew apart at the salesman's question, doing their best not to laugh.

Grace held up her hand. "This one."

"Excellent choice. Have you selected the wedding band to go with it?"

Thorn glanced at Grace, who stifled a laugh, then back at the salesman. "Give us five more minutes and we'll have it done."

Thorn tilted his glass of beer, taking a long swallow, then laughed at another of Josh's jokes. He, Josh, and Tony had closed the garage for a small celebration. Grace had been with him when they'd announced their engagement, then left for her house with plans to return at seven. It gave the boys an hour to party in private. They sat in the office, a cooler filled with beer on the floor.

Tony clasped him on the back. "After all these years, man. I'm happy for you."

"Never thought it would happen, Thorn. Not with the way Wolf's been acting." Reaching down, Josh pulled another beer from the cooler, tossing it to him. "You two set a date?"

"If it were up to me, next week wouldn't be soon enough." Twisting off the cap, Thorn drained a third of the bottle, then set it down. "She wants to tell her parents first, and I need to talk to Del and Boone."

"Your brothers won't give you any grief. They love Grace. We all love Grace." Tony swallowed the last of his beer, tossing the bottle in a nearby can. "You gonna move into her place?"

Thorn thought a moment, then nodded. "Most likely. She owns it and it's bigger than mine. Either of you looking for a place?"

"You looking to sublet yours?" Josh asked. He had a small room above a restaurant in town.

"Or let the landlord know I've got a renter for him. You've seen the place. Two bedrooms, two baths, a small garage." Thorn quoted the amount he paid for rent.

Josh tipped his bottle toward Thorn. "Done. If you move in with Grace, tell the man you've got an exemplary person ready to take over."

Tony shot Thorn a look before they both burst out laughing.

Josh's brows drew together. "What?"

"You don't remember who I'm renting from, do you?"

Scratching his head, Josh scowled, trying to recall. "Guess not."

"Myself...and Del and Boone. It and three other houses on the same block were owned by my parents. Now they're ours."

"Perfect. Do I get the family and friends discount?"

Thorn grinned. "That price *is* the discount, squid."

Josh started to reply when a knock on the front door stopped him.

Thorn glanced at his watch. "That would be Grace. Right on time." Standing, he finished the last of his beer. "Time for you boys to take off."

Tony wiggled his brows. "You and your fiancée have plans for a private celebration?"

Walking to the front, Thorn glanced over his shoulder. "That answer would be above your pay grade, jarhead. Now, get lost."

Opening the front door, Thorn took a moment to let his appreciative gaze wander over Grace. Her dark hair fell in curls around her shoulders, cascading over the yellow blouse clinging to her curves, the tight jeans hugging her hips and legs. Tonight, she wore suede flats, making the top of her head come to the middle of his chest. A perfect fit.

"What's in the basket?" Holding out his hand, he took it from her, then wrapped his other arm around her waist, drawing her in for a kiss. Pulling back, he glanced around, glad to see the street was empty. "Come on inside. This smells too good to let it sit for long. Did you order from Doc's?"

Stopping, she turned toward him. "I'll have you know I cooked what's in there."

"You? I thought all you knew how to do was fix a ham sandwich."

"Shows how much you know about me. There's salad, lasagna, garlic bread, and tiramisu. All made in my kitchen." A self-satisfied grin appeared on her face as she strolled away, heading for the office. "Looks like you were having a party."

"A few beers with Tony and Josh. They're happy for us, by the way." Setting the basket down, he opened the cooler. "We've got beer and, well...more beer."

"A beer would be great. Thanks."

Handing her the bottle, he began to open the basket, then stopped. "Are you sure you don't want to go to my place where we can spread out, relax?"

Taking a sip of her beer, she gazed up at him. "Oh, I definitely want to go to your place—after we eat." Setting the beer down, she walked up to him, wrapping her arms around his neck. "I'm still getting used to all that's happened between us the last few weeks. I thought spending a little time here, where you work, would help me ground myself a little. You know, without a bed being just yards away."

"Whatever you want, sweetheart." Lowering his head, their lips brushed before he deepened the kiss. What started as slow and considerate grew to hungry and demanding as their bodies melded together, their arms tightening around each other. Drawing back, Thorn tucked her head under his chin as he sucked in a breath. "We'd better stop or I might clear off the desk to use as a bed."

"You always were inventive," she teased, moving away to open the basket.

Snapping on two lamps Josh insisted they have, he turned off the overheads, transforming the work area from bright and efficient to quiet and cozy. "Wish I had more comfortable chairs."

"These are fine. Better than in my office." She glanced at him. "Well, my former office." Filling a plate, she handed it to him, along with two slices of garlic bread, then made a plate for herself before sitting down.

"Do you regret it already?" Pulling up a chair next to her, he placed the plate on his lap, taking one of her hands in his.

"Not for an instant. It's as if a giant boulder has been lifted from my shoulders, allowing me to run free. Truthfully, I can't wait to start our new life."

Bringing her hand to his lips, he turned it over, kissing her palm. "It won't be easy."

Love and hope shined in her eyes. "But not nearly as hard as each of us going it alone."

Leaning over, he kissed her. "Not nearly."

An hour passed as they ate, laughed, and talked of their future. Thorn had told the security guard he wouldn't be needed until ten, giving Grace and him time alone, although it still seemed a little odd she wanted to spend the evening at his shop. With all the other obstacles ahead of them, he wasn't about to complain. And now he knew she could cook.

Watching her pack the plates, utensils, and napkins back into the basket, he couldn't help the feeling of complete contentment. Having her back in his life, agreeing to marry him, was more than he deserved. He was determined to never make her regret being with him. Lost in his thoughts, he didn't notice Grace studying him.

"What's going on in your head?" She finished her second beer, feeling better than she had in months...maybe years.

He smirked. "Thinking about all the great meals you'll have waiting for me after a long day of work."

Reaching into the basket, she pulled out a wadded up napkin and threw it at him. "I guess you have a few surprises ahead." She stilled when he grabbed the napkin in midair, then stood, making a move to come after her. "Whoa...hold on..." Skirting around the desk, she feinted in one direction, then another as he stalked toward her.

Grace knew the odds were slim, but she refused to go down without a fight. Dodging his outstretched hand, she squealed when he hooked his arm around her waist.

"You never had a chance." Thorn cupped her face, capturing her mouth, intending to do more when a loud explosion had them jumping apart. "What the..." Before he could finish, Grace dashed out of the office, racing through the back garage to the door, fear surging through him as he called out. "Grace, wait. Don't go out there."

She didn't stop, yelling over her shoulder. "My car's in the back. Call 911."

"Dammit, Grace. Stop."

She didn't hear him as she disappeared outside at the exact moment a second explosion shook the building.

Chapter Fifteen

The force of the second explosion threw Grace against the outside wall of the garage. Pain shot through her shoulder as she lay on the ground, stunned at the sight of her car and Thorn's truck engulfed in flames, unable to believe or process what else she'd seen.

Storming outside, Thorn's heart almost stopped when he saw her, blood trickling down her cheek from a cut on her forehead. Finishing the 911 call, he thrust his phone into his pocket.

"Grace." His panicked voice reached her an instant before he knelt beside her, his hands running over her shoulders, arms, legs, checking for broken bones. "Can you hear me, sweetheart?"

Her dazed eyes met his. "Yes."

"Good." Stripping off his t-shirt, he used it to cover the cut. "What hurts?"

Blinking a few times, she stared at the vehicles, reduced to heaps of burning metal. She thought about the other image she saw, her gut clenching.

Gripping her chin gently, he turned her to face him. "Stay with me, Grace. Are you hurt anywhere else?"

Swallowing a combination of fear and anger, she nodded. "My shoulder." Trying to push herself up, she grimaced, sitting back down.

"Whoa, sweetheart. Stay right where you are." He let out a relieved breath at the sound of approaching sirens. "Paramedics will be here any second."

Thorn glanced around, regret slashing through him at the decision to send the guard away for a few hours. Grace's car and his truck were total losses.

"My father."

Grace's distressed voice tore his gaze away from the scene before him. "What?"

"Wolf. I think he's the one behind this."

Leaning toward her until their faces were inches apart, he put a finger to her lips. "Shhh, sweetheart. You're hurt, scared, and probably angry. Don't say anything you might regret."

"I saw someone running away when I got outside, Thorn." Choking at the smoke, brushing at tears welling in her eyes, she forced herself to continue. "I only got a glimpse of the side of his face, but he was my father's height with dark hair past his collar. He wore a black leather jacket, like the one my father wears. Who else could it be?"

Scrubbing a hand down his face, he shook his head, unwilling to accept her conclusion. "We'll talk about this later."

Paramedics ran up, taking over, as firefighters worked on the burning cars. Standing, staying close, he thought about Grace's words. He couldn't wrap his mind around Wolf doing anything that would endanger his daughter. If it were him, he would have recognized her car, known she was inside. It made no sense.

"We're taking her to the hospital, sir."

Shaking himself, Thorn watched as they placed her on a stretcher, her wide eyes locking with his.

"Thorn?"

Walking beside the paramedics, he touched her arm. "I'm going to the hospital with you."

"Should you call Rick Zoeller?"

He refused to talk about what she thought she saw in front of the people around them. "Grace, I don't think you understand—"

"Sir, you'll have to follow us. There isn't room for you in the ambulance. She'll be in emergency."

Reluctantly, he stepped back, shoving his hands into his pockets as he looked around, relief flooding him when Josh came running up.

"Josh, do you have your truck?"

"Yeah, it's out front." A stream of profanities burst from his mouth when his gaze landed on the burning vehicles. "Where's Grace?"

"On the way to the hospital. I need your keys."

Josh didn't hesitate. "It's across the street. I'll stay here."

"Thanks, man." Running out front, he waved at Tony. "Josh is in the back."

"Where are you..." Tony's words faded away as Thorn jumped into Josh's truck and took off.

"How's Grace?"

Thorn pulled his gaze away from the cold coffee he held in his hand as Rick Zoeller sat down next to him. Strange how your mind worked in a crisis. He'd been through them many times while in Special Forces, dealt with horrific injuries and death. Nothing in his past prepared him for sitting in a waiting room with Grace on the other side of the swinging doors.

"They're still checking her out."

"Did you see her before they brought her in?"

Thorn nodded, a muscle in his jaw twitching at what should've been a celebratory evening. "Yeah. We were together when the explosions happened. She may have dislocated her shoulder, has a cut on her forehead. I don't know what else."

"Explosions?" Without thought, Rick pulled his pen and pad from a pocket.

"Two of them. I figure one was my truck, and the other Grace's car. She ran out right after the first explosion. It's a miracle she wasn't killed."

"Do you know if she saw anything?"

Thorn hesitated. He didn't want to throw suspicion on a man who'd be his father-in-law within a few short weeks. "I'm not sure."

Rick leaned back, stretching his legs out in front of him. "Tell me what you aren't sure about."

"It would be best coming from Grace."

"Who they might not let me see for hours. Meantime, an arsonist may be getting away. Come on, Macklin. Tell me what Grace saw."

Thorn set his cup down and stood, pacing to the window that looked out onto a half-full parking lot. Taking several breaths, he cleared his mind, recalling her words. Turning back to Rick, he crossed his arms, resting his shoulder against the wall.

"It may be nothing, as she was in pain and probably concussed. Anyway, this is what she told me."

Fifteen minutes later, after numerous questions and asking Thorn to repeat what Grace said three times, Rick slid the pad back into his pocket. "Not what I expected."

"My gut tells me it isn't Wolf. He may not be my biggest fan, but he's not going to do something to harm Grace. She has to be mistaken." He'd moved back to the chair next to Rick, growing impatient as the time stretched on. "I'm betting he has an alibi."

"I'll need to speak with Grace, but if she holds to what you told me, I'll have no choice but to bring him in for questioning."

"Mr. Macklin?"

Standing, Thorn walked toward the doctor. "I'm Thorn Macklin. How's Grace?" He glanced at Rick, who moved up beside him.

"A concussion, dislocated shoulder, possible issues with smoke inhalation, and contusions on her face and arms. Nothing life threatening. She'll be fine, but I want to keep her overnight for observation. We're moving her to a private room. Once that's done, you can see her."

"Private room?"

The doctor chuckled. "Her father spoke with the hospital administrator. He's on his way." The man, probably no older than Thorn, narrowed his gaze. "Mr. Jackson said you aren't to see her. Unfortunately for him, she's not a minor and has insisted she wants you in her room. Says you're her fiancé."

"I am. You know, when Wolf gets here, you'll need strong arms to keep him out of her room."

"I've already notified security. Well, I need to check on other patients. I'll stop by her room within a couple hours."

Thorn extended his hand. "Thanks, Doctor."

"Good luck to you, Mr. Macklin."

For once, luck smiled in Thorn's favor. Within thirty minutes, the staff finished moving Grace to her room and summoned him.

He started to follow the nurse, then turned back to Rick. "I hate to leave you out here to face Wolf."

"Actually, this might work in our favor. It'll give me a chance to check out what Grace saw."

"He'll demand to see her."

Rick grinned. "As the good doctor said, she's an adult and asked for you, not him. Mr. Jackson will have to deal with it."

A grim smile crossed Thorn's face before he nodded, following the nurse through the doors. Focusing on the doctor's reassuring description of her injuries, he pushed away his emotions. He knew the importance of staying calm, being in control for Grace's sake. As much as he wanted to pound whoever did this to her, he forced himself to ignore the anger pulsing through him.

"Hey." He walked up to the bed, noting the bandages, tubes, and IV. Nothing he didn't expect.

"Hey." Reaching out, she grasped his hand in as tight a grip as possible given the pain killers they'd insisted she take. "What a way to end an engagement party." Her words were slurred, her eyes glassy.

"It's not over yet, sweetheart. I hear these medical people know how to party." Without letting go of her hand, he grabbed a chair, pulling it up next to the bed. "They treating you okay?"

Trying to smile, she coughed. Placing a hand behind her head, he elevated her enough to ease her discomfort. When she calmed, he laid her head back on the pillow.

"Did they tell you if it's all right to have some water?"

She coughed again, then nodded. "Small sips."

He picked up the plastic cup, bringing the straw to her mouth. "Rick Zoeller is in the waiting area. He wants to talk to you."

"You told him what I saw?"

"Yeah, but you have to remember you were on the ground with a concussion and in pain from your shoulder when you saw the man running away. Implicating your father is a big step."

A commotion in the hall had Thorn opening the door. A nurse, two orderlies, and Rick Zoeller stood in front of Wolf, blocking his path to his daughter's room. Looking over his shoulder at Grace, he closed the door, then walked up to them, not seeing the expected hatred on Wolf's face. Instead, he saw fear, the same as he'd see on the face of any parent whose child had been injured.

"Thorn...you sonofabitch." Red suffused Wolf's face, anger contorting his features.

Holding up his hands, Thorn took a step closer. "It wasn't my decision. Grace decided who she wanted to see."

"You're saying my own daughter doesn't want to see me?" He struggled to get past those blocking his path.

Rick kept his position in front of Wolf. "Mr. Jackson, you've got to calm down. You're not seeing anyone until you do."

Stepping back, Wolf settled fisted hands on his hips, taking a deep breath before looking at Thorn. "How is she?"

"She's in pain, confused and groggy from the painkillers." Thorn rubbed the back of his neck. "We were together when the first explosion happened. She wanted to be sure I wasn't hurt. Give her a little time, then she'll be ready to see you."

The nurse shifted her gaze from Thorn to Wolf. "You should listen to her fiancé, sir. She needs to rest. You aren't going to help with the way you're feeling right now."

Wolf's eyes widened, his jaw going slack. "Fiancé?" A vein in his neck pulsed as he locked his gaze on Thorn. "You and Grace?"

Thorn blew out a breath. This wasn't how they'd planned to tell Wolf of their engagement. "It happened last night. The only people who know are standing in this hall, plus Josh and Tony. She planned to tell you and her mother tomorrow."

Color drained from Wolf's face, his shoulders sagging as the will to fight dissolved. Looking at the ground, he shook his head. "It never should've played out this way." Regret laced his voice, sorrow replacing the rage of a few moments before.

Thorn didn't know how to interpret Wolf's statement and didn't want to discuss it any further in the hall. "I'm going to go back into the room. Why don't you go to the waiting area and I'll come out in a little bit. We need to talk." He looked at Rick, wondering if the detective had said anything about what Grace saw.

"Come on, Mr. Jackson. I'll sit out there with you." Rick stepped closer, nodding toward the doors behind them.

"I want to see her, Thorn."

"I know, Wolf. I'll talk to her. It's all I can promise right now."

Letting out a slow breath, Wolf nodded, then turned away.

"Give me a minute, Mr. Jackson." Rick stepped closer to Thorn, keeping his voice low. "I didn't go into any details of what Grace saw, but since it took him a while to get here, I asked Wolf about where he was tonight. Turns out he was at a business dinner with the Chamber of Commerce, then stayed for drinks with a few members. It'll be easy to check out."

"So it's not him."

"Not if what he told me holds up, which I think it will. The man ran into the hospital, panicked at the message he got about Grace. He'd have to be a terrific actor to hide how scared he felt."

"Yeah, it's what I expected." Thorn thought a minute, his lips drawing into a thin line. "Grace did see someone."

"I don't doubt it. She gave too much detail not to have seen someone running away. It just wasn't her father." Hearing his phone, Rick pulled it from his pocket, checking the caller ID. "It's your brother."

Thorn grabbed his own phone, seeing Del had called several times. Mumbling an oath, he remembered how he'd muted it when he entered the hospital.

Rick glanced at him as he spoke with Del. "Got it. Right. I'll meet you at the station. Give me thirty minutes to finish up here. Thanks, Sheriff." His mouth twisted in grim satisfaction.

"What is it?"

"Turns out your security guard got there in time to see someone running away. He jumped in his car and followed the guy. His boss called Del, who happened to be on the same highway and joined the chase. They're taking him to the police station for questioning."

Thorn's tense features began to relax. "You think he's the man?"

"Del said they found gas, motor oil, and some other paraphernalia in the trunk of his car. So yes, I think there's a good chance he's our guy." Extending his hand, he grasped Thorn's. "I need to get moving. Keep an eye on our girl." He turned to walk away.

"*My* girl, Zoeller," Thorn called after him.

Lifting a hand, Rick glanced over his shoulder. "Details."

Rick sat in a small room at the police station with Thorn, Del, and Boone, scanning the paperwork on the last fire. "Crayton Jones. Do any of you recognize it?"

Thorn closed his eyes, scratching the stubble on his chin. "I know that name."

"About two hundred pounds, five feet ten, hair to his collar, wearing a leather jacket." Rick rifled through the paperwork for more information. "Sixty-four, Vietnam vet."

Thorn snapped his fingers. "That's it. Do you have a picture?"

"Just the one when we booked him." Rick slid the file over.

Thorn studied the image as Del and Boone moved closer to look over his shoulder. "That's the guy. He came by the shop when we opened. Said he knew our father. Either of you ever hear of him?"

Del and Boone shook their heads. "I don't recall Pop ever mentioning a Crayton Jones," Del said.

"According to Mom, he had several buddies he stayed in contact with after the war." Boone took one more look at the photo, then sat back in his chair. "He lost touch with most of them over the years."

Del leaned forward, resting his arms on the table. "Did he give you any indication why he started the fires?"

"He raged on quite a bit. The old-timers here at the jail think he's got some mental issues, maybe PTSD. Regardless, he kept saying something about being cheated out of money and you owed him." Shrugging, he dragged the folder back across the desk. "As quick as he talked, he clammed up. Asked for a lawyer."

Thorn, Del, and Boone exchanged glances, none of them responding.

Rick closed the file, crossing his arms. "Look, if any of you have an idea of what he's talking about, I need to know."

Del ran a hand through his hair, letting out a ragged breath. "After our parents died, we found some documents about business dealings. No names, identifying data, or dates, although some showed amounts. Nothing to identify what happened or who was involved. None of the businesses were named and there weren't any addresses. From what we saw, some of the transactions went south."

Boone sat forward. "The paperwork was a mess, with information scratched out, then changed. When we saw it, the last entry was over twenty years old."

"Where's all the paperwork now?" Rick asked.

"That's the thing. We locked it in a shed near the barn. It's where our parents kept a lot of old stuff." Boone shifted in the chair, shaking his head. "The whole building went up in flames a few years ago during a huge lightning storm. We lost everything."

"Convenient," Rick mumbled.

Del stood, glaring down at him. "You've got something to say, just say it. I guarantee it's probably nothing we haven't already thought or cursed our father about."

"Sit down, Del. I hate dead ends, that's all." Strumming his fingers on the table, Rick seemed to be trying to settle things in his mind. Standing, he picked up the file. "Whatever went down with your father has no bearing on you three."

"And Jones?" Thorn asked.

"We've got him on arson and various other charges. A good lawyer might be able to convince the judge of mental illness. Either way, he'll serve time somewhere."

"Family?" Del asked.

"Not that we know of."

"I know this might be asking a lot, but keep me informed about how this case is going." Del looked at Thorn, then Boone.

"Not a problem at all, Sheriff." Rick smiled. "I'm all for interagency cooperation."

Once outside, Thorn clasped Del's shoulder. "I know what you're thinking, bro, and I'm with you on it."

"I think we need to consider it." Del reached into his pocket, pulling out the keys to his truck.

"Either of you want to share what you're talking about?" Boone pushed his cowboy hat low on his forehead, crossing his arms.

"Helping with attorney fees for Jones." Del glanced around, glad for a few minutes of privacy. "What are the chances of a man showing up in Whiskey Bend, being an old army buddy of Pop's, and torching Thorn's place because he said we owe him money?"

"Could all be unrelated."

"I know, Boone. That's why we don't have to make a decision now. Rick will keep us informed of how it's going, then we can decide. It's just something I think we should consider."

Boone nodded. "I hear you, and agree. Sins of our father and all that."

Thorn snorted. "Yeah, something like that."

"When does Grace go home?" Del's mouth tipped up at the corners.

Thorn returned his grin. "Today. I'm headed there now. Moving into her place this weekend."

Boone punched him in the arm. "I'm glad for you two. When's the wedding?"

"Soon. Real soon."

Epilogue

"When Thorn said the wedding would be soon, I didn't think he meant within a couple weeks." Boone tilted the glass of beer to his lips. "Grace isn't even healed yet."

Del chuckled. "I doubt her injuries make any difference to Thorn. They aren't going on a honeymoon for a few months, and he's swamped with work. They didn't lose a single client because of the fires, and from what Tony says, they're getting more inquiries every day."

Thorn and Grace had chosen their favorite place, the park a few blocks from downtown, for their reception. When Thorn helped her out of the truck, the first thing she spotted was the Harley he'd been working on non-stop since the last fire. Her stunned shriek caught most everyone by surprise. If her shoulder had been healed, Del believed she might have jumped on the bike and taken it for a spin, leaving the guests behind.

"Gentlemen." Kull walked up and tilted his bottle toward them. "Quite a party. Close to half the town is here."

"Which reminds me, I see Shane and Alley at the refreshment table. I want to find out how Mason's rehab is coming." Boone finished his beer, setting the empty bottle on a tray. "Doc Johnson is okay, but with him retiring, I'd rather work with Mason. I'll catch up with you two later."

"Hard to believe Thorn and Grace made it work after all this time. It was a helluva journey he went on before deciding to come home. I'm glad Wolf decided to support their decision and her change of profession." Pondering his drink, Kull shifted toward Del, a devilish grin on his face. "One down. That leaves you and Boone."

Del choked on his drink, swiping an arm across his mouth. "Geez, Kull. What made you say something so ridiculous?"

"You boys aren't getting any younger. With Thorn tying the knot, it makes sense the two of you would start thinking about it."

"Not even a little. I'm still a young man with a lot of women to roll through."

Kull laughed. "Right. I hear you haven't been seen with a woman in months. Many months, if rumors are true."

Del groaned. "Just one more problem with being the sheriff in a small town. I like my privacy and I sure can't get any here. Not if everyone keeps tabs on my activities."

"So spread your wings, son. Missoula isn't that far away, and no one is bound to see you."

"I can't believe you're giving me dating advice, Kull. Aren't you the one who said women are more trouble than they're worth?"

Kull lowered his voice. "Shhh, Del. I don't want any of the ladies to hear you. Besides, I may have been a little hasty in my opinion."

Del's brows furrowed, but he didn't have a chance to respond.

"What are you two chatting about?" Thorn extended his hand, his other wrapped around his bride's waist.

"Nothing." Del spoke before Kull had a chance. Still, it didn't stop the older man.

"Talking about who is next. Del or Boone."

Grace winked at him. "You know, Kull, I was thinking the same."

"Ah, hell. Not you, too. I need another beer." Del stalked off, hearing the laughter behind him.

Kull crossed his arms. "I give him a year before the right woman changes his mind."

"I'm thinking two," Thorn responded.

"I think you're both wrong." Grace's smug expression had Thorn wondering what she knew that he didn't. "My guess is the single life of our sheriff will be a lot less than one or two years." She chuckled at their disbelieving expressions. "And I doubt he'll know what hit him."

Two fractured hearts. One chance to correct the mistakes from their past. Will Del ignore the warnings and seize the choice taken from him years before? Start reading Del's story to find out!

If you want to keep current on all my preorders, new releases, and other happenings, sign up for my newsletter at: http://www.shirleendavies.com/contact-me.html

A Note from Shirleen

Thank you for taking the time to read **Thorn**!

If you enjoyed it, please consider telling your friends or posting a short review. Word of mouth is an author's best friend and much appreciated.

I care about quality, so if you find something in error, please contact me via email at shirleen@shirleendavies.com

Books by Shirleen Davies

Contemporary Western Romance Series
MacLarens of Fire Mountain

Second Summer, Book One
Hard Landing, Book Two
One More Day, Book Three
All Your Nights, Book Four
Always Love You, Book Five
Hearts Don't Lie, Book Six
No Getting Over You, Book Seven
'Til the Sun Comes Up, Book Eight
Foolish Heart, Book Nine

Macklins of Whiskey Bend

Thorn, Book One
Del, Book Two
Boone, Book Three

Historical Western Romance Series
Redemption Mountain

Redemption's Edge, Book One
Wildfire Creek, Book Two
Sunrise Ridge, Book Three
Dixie Moon, Book Four

Survivor Pass, Book Five
Promise Trail, Book Six
Deep River, Book Seven
Courage Canyon, Book Eight
Forsaken Falls, Book Nine
Solitude Gorge, Book Ten
Rogue Rapids, Book Eleven
Angel Peak, Book Twelve
Restless Wind, Book Thirteen
Storm Summit, Book Fourteen
Mystery Mesa, Book Fifteen
Thunder Valley, Book Sixteen
A Very Splendor Christmas, Holiday Novella, Book
Seventeen
Paradise Point, Book Eighteen,
Silent Sunset, Book Nineteen
Rocky Basin, Book Twenty, Coming Next in the Series!

MacLarens of Fire Mountain

Tougher than the Rest, Book One
Faster than the Rest, Book Two
Harder than the Rest, Book Three
Stronger than the Rest, Book Four
Deadlier than the Rest, Book Five
Wilder than the Rest, Book Six

MacLarens of Boundary Mountain

Colin's Quest, Book One,
Brodie's Gamble, Book Two
Quinn's Honor, Book Three
Sam's Legacy, Book Four
Heather's Choice, Book Five
Nate's Destiny, Book Six
Blaine's Wager, Book Seven
Fletcher's Pride, Book Eight
Bay's Desire, Book Nine
Cam's Hope, Book Ten

Romantic Suspense

Eternal Brethren, Military Romantic Suspense

Steadfast, Book One
Shattered, Book Two
Haunted, Book Three
Untamed, Book Four
Devoted, Book Five
Faithful, Book Six
Exposed, Book Seven
Undaunted, Book Eight
Resolute, Book Nine
Unspoken, Book Ten
Defiant, Book Eleven
Consumed, Book Twelve, Coming Next in the Series!

Peregrine Bay, Romantic Suspense

Reclaiming Love, Book One
Our Kind of Love, Book Two
Edge of Love, Book Three, Coming Next in the Series!

Find all of my books at:
https://www.shirleendavies.com/books.html

About Shirleen

Shirleen Davies writes romance—historical, contemporary, and romantic suspense. She grew up in Southern California, attended Oregon State University, and has degrees from San Diego State University and the University of Maryland. Her real passion is writing emotionally charged stories of flawed people who find redemption through love and acceptance. She now lives with her husband in a beautiful town in northern Arizona.

I love to hear from my readers!

Send me an email: shirleen@shirleendavies.com
Visit my Website: https://www.shirleendavies.com/
Sign up to be notified of New Releases:
https://www.shirleendavies.com/contact/
Follow me on Amazon:
http://www.amazon.com/author/shirleendavies
Follow me on BookBub:
https://www.bookbub.com/authors/shirleen-davies

Other ways to connect with me:

Facebook Author Page:
http://www.facebook.com/shirleendaviesauthor
Pinterest: http://pinterest.com/shirleendavies
Instagram:
https://www.instagram.com/shirleendavies_author/
TikTok: shirleendavies_author
Twitter: www.twitter.com/shirleendavies

Avalanche Ranch Press, LLC
PO Box 12618
Prescott, AZ 86304